Stinging Fly Patrons

Many thanks to Ann Barry, Denise Blake, Trish Byrne, Bruce Carolan, Edmund Condon, Liam Cusack, Wendy Donegan, Garret Fitzgerald, Michael Gillen, Helene Gurian, Jim Hannon, James Jameson, Claire Keegan, Jerry Kelleher, Conor Kennedy, Ruth Kenny, Gráinne Killeen, Susan Knight, Joe Lawlor, Irene Rose Ledger, David Lyons, Petra McDonough, Micéal McGovern, Lynn Mc Grane, Finbar McLoughlin, Maggie McLoughlin, Dan McMahon, Ama, Grace & Fraoch Mac Sweeney, Mary McSweeney, Orna McSweeney, Paddy & Moira McSweeney, Helen Monaghan, Christine Monk, Críona Ní Gháirbhí, Barry O'Brien, Maura O'Brien, Joseph O'Connor, Mary O'Donnell, Nessa O'Mahony, Padraig O'Neill, Marie O'Sullivan, Peter J. Pitkin, Kieran Plunkett, Kevin Robinson, Ronan Rose-Roberts, Fiona Ruff, Eileen Sheridan, Brian Smyth, Peter Smyth, Karen, Conor & Rowan Sweeney, Mike Timms, Olive Towey, Font Literary Agency & Writing Centre, Munster Literature Centre, Poetry Ireland, Trashface Books and the White House Poets.

We'd also like to thank those individuals who have expressed the preference to remain anonymous.

By making an annual contribution of just 50 euro, patrons provide the magazine and press with vital support and encouragement.

Become a patron online at
www.stingingfly.org
or send a cheque or postal order to:
The Stinging Fly, PO Box 6016, Dublin 8.

issue 16/volume two
Summer 2010

NEW FICTION

ESSAY

FEATURED POETS

NEW POEMS

'... God has specially appointed me to this city, so as though it were a large thoroughbred horse which because of its great size is inclined to be lazy and needs the stimulation of some stinging fly...'
—Plato, *The Last Days of Socrates*

Next Issue Due: October 2010

The Stinging Fly
New Writers, New Writing

Guest Editor
Sean O'Reilly

Poetry Editor
Eabhan Ní Shúileabháin

Design & Layout
Fergal Condon

Managing Editor
Declan Meade

Assistant Editor
Emily Firetog

Webmaster
Aiden O'Reilly

Readers: Tina Brescanu, Claire Coughlan, Conor Farnan, Tom Mathews

© Copyright remains with authors and artists, 2010
Printed by Beta Print Services, County Meath

ISBN 978-1-906539-14-6 ISSN 1393-5690

Published three times a year (February, June and October). We operate an open submission policy. Submissions are accepted from January to March each year. Full guidelines are on our website: www.stingingfly.org

The Stinging Fly gratefully acknowledges the support of The Arts Council/ An Chomhairle Ealaíon and Dublin City Council.

Editorial

It's a bit of a kinky business being an editor of a literary magazine—especially when you are the guest editor. You're not staying long and the rules are unclear. The bedroom is haunted. You have to read a lot of stuff which is 'unpublished.' There are piles and piles of it, short stories and poems and other stuff there's no name for—as yet. And all this stuff, this unpublished writing, has a soft secret quality, an occult nakedness, a raw kind of before-ness. Like gifts. The opposite of already. Like dreams. And just as when somebody gets it into their head to tell you one of their own, you listen hard to what is said, to what is avoided, disguised and summarised. Although you can't be sure what any of it means, you start to ask yourself what is it to tell a dream well and what is really going on when a dream is told badly and, of course, why is this person driven to share this dream? Because all this stuff to be read shares the desire to be transformed. Idealised. It yearns to be published. It hopes to exist. To happen. It is afraid of its own disappearance, its radical uselessness. Like a lover, it waits. And waits.

A shy lover. An editor grows kinky on the shyness of these dreams. The editor is an audience of one before a stage where the dancer blushes halfway through and runs behind the curtain wriggling with embarrassment. If writing is a bit like a pole dance, then the pole is Place. The pole is usually rammed deep into the reliable muck of the countryside because the foundations of the city seem to be made of sand. Nobody is dancing in the city it seems. Most of the dancers, following some kind of unwritten rule, begin with a swish of the old greasy feather boa of the Weather—that's what comes off first. But before too long, the blushes begin, the anxiety turns to awkwardness, stiffness and then they cut their losses and make a run for it. And the editor can be left staring at the rust and fading fingerprints on the pious metal pole, wondering about the history of shyness in Ireland.

Sean O'Reilly
Dublin, June 2010

Sean O'Reilly is the author of *Curfew and other stories*, the novels *Love and Sleep* and *The Swing of Things*, and *Watermark* (with The Stinging Fly Press.) He lives in Dublin.

NEWS

Comhchealg

As well as sporting a new look, our summer issue sees the arrival of Comhchealg (p. 100-103), a new section to the magazine which is dedicated to Irish-language poetry alongside translations into English. Aifric Mac Aodha is our first featured writer and from now on, she will act as the magazine's Irish-language poetry editor. Submissions are being accepted up until the end of June for future editions.

Treoirlínte:

- Ní léifear aon dán ríomhsheolta. Seoltar na hiarratais chuig: Aifric Mac Aodha, Eagarthóir Filíochta, The Stinging Fly, Bosca PO 6016, BÁC 8.

- Ní léifear ach ceithre dhán ar a mhéad

- Ní léifear ach dánta fiche líne nó níos gonta

- Bíodh litir mhínithe leis an iarratas agus seoladh r-phoist luaite inti ar mhaithe le comhfhreagras. Más mian leat go gcuirfí d'iarratas ar ais chugat, bíodh clúdach faoi stampa agus seoladh istigh leis.

Novel Workshop 2010-2011

Sean O'Reilly will lead a second 'New Way to Fly' novel-writing workshop later this year. The workshop runs over a period of twenty weeks (starting in October) with weekly sessions where participants present and discuss their own work. In addition there will be five day-long sessions with visiting writers. Eight to ten participants will be selected on the basis of work submitted and they will be expected to work towards the completion of the first draft of a novel. To receive more information on this year's workshop, send an e-mail to stingingfly@gmail.com.

Sharp Sticks, Driven Nails

Next up from the Stinging Fly Press is an anthology of new short stories edited by Philip Ó Ceallaigh. The book will be published in October and among the authors included are writers from Ireland, Romania, Serbia, Russia, Israel, Malaysia, New Zealand and the US. The title *Sharp Sticks, Driven Nails* derives from the book of Ecclesiastes.

Philip Ó Ceallaigh has been contributing to the magazine since 2000. He has published two short story collections: *Notes from a Turkish Whorehouse* (2006) and *The Pleasant Light of Day* (2009).

A Modest Proposal

Modesty Press is a new independent publisher based in Dublin and this year they hope to publish the first volume of *A Modest Review*, a quarterly journal of new writing. To this end they are currently seeking submissions of short fiction, poetry, and creative non-fiction.

Submissions should be sent to Modesty Press, 25-26 Windsor Place, Pembroke St. Lower, Dublin 2. Submissions can also be made electronically (in either .pdf or .rtf format) to submissions@modestypress.com. Please note however that hardcopy submissions will receive priority.

—www.modestypress.com

The Poetry Bus

Isn't it always the way? You stand around waiting for ages and then two or three of them come rumbling along at once.

Climb aboard *The Poetry Bus* magazine, first issue due to pull in sometime this month (June 2010). For full timetable and fare information, see http://thepoetrybus.blogspot.com/.

Claire Keegan Workshop

Claire Keegan (*Antartica, Walk The Blue Fields)* is running a residential writing workshop over the weekend of August 6th to 8th, aimed at people who are just starting out at writing fiction. All who have an interest in learning how fiction works and want to put pen to paper will be welcome.

The workshop will take place at the Innisfree International College & Convention Centre on the shores of Lough Gill in County Sligo. Another workshop for more advanced writers will take place later in the year. For further information, contact ckworkshops@yahoo.co.uk.

Sites of Possible Interest

In no particular order…

www.wordlegs.com
www.milkandcookiestories.com
www.ubu.com
www.theirishstory.com
www.librarything.com
http://irishpublishingnews.com/

Stay Informed

Sign up to our e-mail newsletter or join **The Stinging Fly Group** on **Facebook** for regular updates about all our publications, events and activities.

The Singing Fly Cafe

for lively online discussion and debate
www.stingingfly.org/discussion/

UPCOMING DEADLINES

July 30
Essex 10th Open Poetry Competition
www.essex-poetry-festival.co.uk

July 31
Sean O'Faoláin Short Story Competition
www.munsterlit.ie

August 3
Over The Edge New Writer of the Year
overtheedgeliteraryevents.blogspot.com

August 6
The Manchester Poetry Prize
www.manchesterwritingcompetition.co.uk

August 13
Dromineer Literary Festival Prizes
www.dromineerliteraryfestival.ie

September 24
Patrick Kavanagh Poetry Award
www.patrickkavanaghcountry.com

FESTIVAL DATES

July 4 - 10
West Cork Literary Festival
www.westcorkliteraryfestival.ie

July 10 - 18
Kinsale Arts Festival
www.kinsaleartsweek.com

July 14 - 18
SoundEye Festival
www.soundeye.org

July 12 - 25
Galway Arts Festival
www.galwayartsfestival.ie

September 15 - 19
Frank O'Connor Short Story Festival
www.munsterlit.ie

September 22 - 26
ASPECTS Irish Literature Festival
www.aspectsfestival.co.uk

October 7 - 10
Dromineer Literary Festival
www.dromineerliteraryfestival.ie

Kennedy

Desmond Hogan

A nineteen-year-old youth is made to dig a shallow grave in waste ground beside railway tracks near Limerick bus station and then shot with an automatic pistol.

Eyes blue-green, brown-speckled, of blackbird's eggs.

He wears a hoodie jacket patterned with attack helicopters.

Murdered because he was going to snitch—go to the guards about a murder he'd witnessed—his friend Cuzzy had fired the shot. The victim had features like a western stone wall. The murder vehicle—a stolen cobalt Ford Kuga—set on fire at Ballyneety near Lough Gur.

The hesitant moment by Lough Gur when blackthorn blossom and hawthorn blossom are unrecognisable from one another, the one expiring, the other coming into blossom.

Creeping willow grows in the waste ground near Limerick bus station—as it was April male catskins yellow, with pollen, on separate trees small greenish female stamens. In April also whitlow grass which Kennedy's grandmother Evie used to cure inflammation near fingernails and toenails.

In summer creeping cinquefoil grows in the waste ground.

He was called Kennedy by Michaela, his mother, after John F. Kennedy, and Edward Kennedy, both of whom visited this city, the latter with a silver dollar haircut and tie with small knot and square ends. He must have brought a large jar of Brylcreem with him, Kennedy's father, Bongo, remarked about him.

'When I was young and comely,
Sure, good fortune on me shone,
My parents loved me tenderly.'

A pious woman found Saint Sebastian's body in a sewer and had a dream he told her to bury him in the Catacombs.

Catacumbas. Late Latin word. Latin of Julian the Apostate who studied the Gospels and then returned to the Greek gods.

The Catacombs. A place to take refuge in. A place to scratch prayers on the wall in. A place to paint in.

Cut into porous tufa rock, they featured wall paintings such as one of three officials whom Nebuchadnezzar flung in the furnace for not bowing before a golden image of him in the plain of Dura in Babylon but who were spared.

Three officials, arms outstretched, in pistachio-green jester's apparel amid flames of maple red.

The body of Sebastian the Archer refused death by arrows and he had to be beaten to death. Some have surmised the arrows were symbolic and he was raped.

As the crime boss brought Kennedy to be murdered he told a story:

'I shook hands with Bulldog who is as big as a Holstein Friesian and who has fat cheeks.

'It was Christmas and we got a crate and had a joint.

'He said "I have the stiffness."

'He slept in the same bed as me in the place I have in Ballysimon.

'In the morning he says "Me chain is gone and it was a good chain. I got it in Port Mandel near Manchester."

'He pulled up all the bedclothes.

'He says "I'll come back later and if I don't get me chain your Lexus with the wind down roof will be gone."

'He came back later but he saw the squad car—"the scum bags," he said—and he went away.

'A week later I saw Cocka, a hardy young fellow, with Bulldog's chain, in Sullivan's Lane.'

The crime boss, who is descended from the Black and Tans, himself wears a white-gold chain from Crete, an American gold ring large as a Spanish grandee's ring, a silver bomber jacket and pointy shoes of true white.

He has a stack of nude magazines in his house in Ballysimon, offers you custard and creams from a plate with John Paul II's—Karol Wojtyla's—head on it, plays Country and Western a lot.

Sean Wilson—Blue Hills of Breffni, Westmeath Bachelor.

Sean Moore—Dun Laoghaire can be such a Lonely Place.

Johnny Cash—I Walk the Line.

Ballysimon is famed for a legitimate dumping site but some people are given money to dump rubbish in alternative ways. Millionaires from dumping rubbish, it is said of them.

By turning to violence, to murder, they create a history, they create a style for themselves. The become Ikons as ancient as Calvary.

Matthew tells us his Roman solder torturers put a scarlet robe on Christ, Mark and John—a robe of purple.

Emerging from a garda car Kennedy's companion and accomplice Cuzzy, in a grey pinstripe jersey, is surprised into history.

Centurion's facial features. A flick of hair to the right above his turf cut makes him a little like a crested grebe.

South Hill boys like Cuzzy are like the man-eating mares of King Diomedes of the Bistones that Hercules was entrusted to capture—one of the twelve labours King Eurystheus imposed on him.

'If I had to choose between Auschwitz and here,' he says of his cell, 'I'd choose Auschwitz.'

As Kennedy's body is brought to Janesboro church some of his brothers clasp their hands in attitudes of prayer. Others simply drop their heads in grief.

Youths in suits with chest hammer pleats and cigarette-rolled shoulders. Mock-snakeskin shoes. With revolver cufflinks.

One of the brothers has a prison tattoo—three Chinese letters in biro and ink—on the side of his right ear.

The youngest brother is the only one to demur jacket and tie, has his white shirt hanging over his trousers and wears a silver chain with boxing gloves.

Michaela's—Kennedy's mother—hair is pêle-mêle blanche-blonde, she wears horn-toed, fleur de lys patterned, lace up black high heels, mandorala—oval—ring, ruby and gold diamante on fingernails against her black.

Her businessman boyfriend wears a Saville-Row-style suit chosen from his wardrobe of dark lilac suits, grey and black lounge suits, suits with black collars, wine suits, plum jackets, claret-red velvet one-button jackets.

Kennedy's father Bongo had been a man with kettle-black eyebrows, who was familiar with the juniper berries and the rowan berries and the scarlet berries of the bittersweet—the woody nightshade—sequestered his foal with magpie face and Talmud scholar's beard where these berries, some healing, some poisonous, were abundant. He knew how to challenge the witch's broom.

John Joe Criggs, the umbrella mender in Killeely, used send boys who looked like potoroos—rat kangaroos and prehensile tails—to Weston where they lived, looking for spare copper.

'You're as well hung as a stallion like your father,' Bongo would say to Kennedy. 'Get a partner.'

In Clare for the summer he once turned to Michaela in the night in Kilrush during a fight.

'Go into the Kincora Hotel and get a knife so I can kill this fellow.'

He always took Kennedy to Ballyheigue at Marymass—September 8—where people in bare feet took water in bottles from the Holy Well, left scapulars, names and photographs of people who were dead, children who'd been killed.

He fell in a pub fight. Never woke up.

His mother Evie had hung herself when they settled her.

Hair ivory grey at edges, then sienna, in a ponytail tied by velvet ribbon, usually in tattersal coat, maxi skirt, heelless sandals.

On the road she'd loved to watch the mistle thrush who came to Ireland with the Act of Union of 1800, the Wee Willie Wagtail—blue tit—with black eyestrips and lemon breast, the chaffinch with pink lightings on its breast who would come up close to you, in winter the *frochán*—ring ouzel, white crescent around its breast, bird of river, of crags.

On the footbridge at Doonas near Clondara she told Kennedy of the two Jehovah's Witnesses who were assaulted in Clondara, their bibles burned, the crowd cheered on by the Parish Priest, and then the Jehovah's Witnesses bound to the peace in court for blasphemy.

Michaela's father Billser had been in Glin Industrial School. The Christian Brothers, with Abbey School of Acting voices, used get them to strip naked and lash them with the cat of nine tails. Boys with smidgen penises. A dust, a protest of pubic hair. Boys with pubes as red as the fox who came to steal the sickly chickens, orange as the beak of an Aylesbury duck, brown of the tawny owl.

Then bring them to the Shannon when the tide was in and force them to immerse in salt water.

The Shannon food—haws, dulse, barnacles—they ate them. They robbed mangels, turnips. They even robbed the pigs' and bonhams'—piglets'—food.

'You have eyes like the blackbird's eggs. You have eys like the céirseach's eggs. You have eyes like the merie's eggs,' a Brother, nicknamed the Seabhac—hawk—used tell Billser.

Blue-green, brown-speckled.

He was called the Seabhac because he used to ravage boys the way the hawk makes a sandwich of autumn brood pigeons or meadow pipits, leaving a flush of feathers.

He had ginger-beer hirsute like the ruffous-barred sparrowhawk that quickly gives up when it misses a target, lays eggs in abandoned crows' nests.

A second reason for his nickname was because he was an expert in Irish and the paper-covered Irish dictionary was penned by an Seabhac—the Hawk.

Father Edward J. Flanagan from Ballymoe, North Galway, who founded Boys Town in Omaha and was played by Spencer Tracy, came to Ireland in 1946 and visited Glin Industrial School.

The Seabhac gave him a patent hen's egg, tea in a cup with blackbirds on it, Dundee cake on a plate with the same pattern.

Billser used cry salty tears when he remembered Glin.

Michael's grandfather Torrie had been in the British Army and the old British names for places in Limerick City kept breaking into his conversation—Lax Weir, Patrick Punch Corner, Saint George's Street.

Cuzzy and Kennedy met at a Palaestra—boxing club.

Cuzzy was half-Brazilian.

'My father was Brazilian. He knocked my mother and went away.'

'Are you riding any woman now?' he asked Kennedy, who had rabbit-coloured pubes, in the showers.

'You have nipples like monkey fingers,' Kennedy said to Cuzzy, who has palomino-coloured pubes, in the showers.

The coach, who looked like a pickled onion with tattoos in the nude was impugned for messing with the teenage boxers. HIV Lips was his nickname.

'Used box for CIE Boxing Club,' he said of himself. 'Would go around the country. They used wear pink-lined vests, and I says no way am I going wear that.'

'He sniffed my jocks. And there were no stains on them,' a shaven headed boxer who looked like a defurred monkey or a peeled banana, reported in denunciation of him.

A man who had a grudge against him used scourge a statue of the Greek boxer Theagenes of Thasos until it fell on him, killing him.

The statue was thrown in the sea and fished up by fishermen.

In the Palaestra was a poster of John Cena with leather wrappings on his forearm like the Terme Boxer—Pugile delle Terme—a first century BC copy of a second century BC statue which depicted Theagenes of Thasos.

John Cena in a black baseball cap, briefs showing above trousers beside a lingering poster for Circus Vegas at Two Mile Inn—a kick boxer in mini-bikini briefs and mock-crocodile boots.

Kennedy and Cuzzy were brought to the Garda Station one night when they were walking home from the Boxing Club.

'They'll take anyone in tracksuits.'

Cuzzy, aged sixteen, was thrown in the girls' cell.

Kennedy was thumped with a map lamp, a telephone book used to prevent his body from being bruised.

Cuzzy was thumped with a baton through a towel with soap in it.

A black guard put his tongue in Kennedy's ear. A Polish guard felt his genitals.

Kennedy punched the Polish guard and was jailed.

Solicitors brought parcels of heroin and cocaine into jail.

Youths on parole would swallow one eighth heroin and fifty euro bags of heroin, thus sneak them in.

One youth put three hundred diazepam, three hundred steroid, three ounces of citric in a bottle, three needles up his anus.

Túr, Cant for anus.

Ríspún, Cant for jail.

Slop out in mornings.

Not even granule coffee for breakfast. Something worse.

Locked up most of the day.

One youth with a golf-ball face, skin-coloured lips of the young Dickie Rock, when his baseball cap was removed, a pronounced bald patch on his blond head, had a parakeet in his cell.

Cuzzy would bring an adolescent Alsatian to the Unemployment Office.

Then he and Kennedy got a job laying slabs near the cement factory at Raheen.

Apart from work, Limerick routine.

Drugs in cling-foil or condoms put up their anuses, guards stopping them—fingers up their anuses.

Tired of the routine they both went to Donegal to train with AC armalite rifles and machine guns in fields turned salmon-colour by ragged robin.

The instructor had a Vietnam veteran pepper and salt beard and wore Stars and Stripes plimsolls.

The farmer who used own the house they stayed in would have a boy come for one month in the summer from an Industrial School, by arrangement with the Brothers.

The boy used sleep in the same bed as him and the farmer made him wear girl's knickers.

In Kennedy's room was a poster of Metallica—fuschine bikini top, mini-bikini, skull locket on forehead, fuschine mouth, belly button that looked like a deep cleavage of buttocks, skeleton's arms about her.

'It was on Bermuda's island
That I met with Captain Moore…'

'It's like the Albanians. They give you a bit of rope with a knot at the top.

'Bessa they call it.

'They will kill you or one of your family.

'You know the Albanians by the ears. Their ears are taped back at birth.

'And they have dark eyebrows.

'I was raised on the Island.

'You could leave your doors open. They were the nicest people.

'Drugs spoiled people.'

Weston where Kennedy grew up was like Bedford-Stuyvesant or Brownsville New

York where Mike Tyson grew up, his mother, who died when he was sixteen, regularly observing him coming home with clothes he didn't pay for.

Kennedy once took a €150 tag off a golf club in a Limerick store, replaced it with a €20 tag, and paid for it.

As a small boy he had a Staffordshire terrier called Daisy.

Eyes a blue coast watch, face a sea of freckles, he let the man from Janseboro who sucked little boys' knobs buy him 99s—the ice-cream cones with chocolate flake stuck in them, syrup on top, or traffic-light cakes—cakes with scarlet and green jellies on the icing.

He'd play knocker gawlai—knock at doors in Weston and run away.

He'd throw eggs at taxis.

Once a taxi driver chased him with a baseball bat.

'I smoked twenty cigarettes since I was eleven.

'Used work as a mechanic part-time then.

'I cut it down to ten and then to five recently. My doctor told me my lungs were black and I'd be on an oxygen mask by the time I was twenty.

'I'm nineteen.'

The youth in the petrol-blue jacket spoke against the Island on which someone on a bicycle was driving horses.

A lighted motorbike was going up and down Island Field.

We were on the Metal Bridge side of the Shannon.

It was late afternoon, mid-December.

'They put barbed wire under the Metal Bridge to catch the bodies that float down. A boy jumped off the bridge, got caught in the barbed wire and was drowned.

'They brought seventeen stolen cars here one day and burned all of them.'

There were three cars in the water now, one upside down, with the wheels above the tide.

'When I was a child my mother used always be saying "I promised Our Lady of Lourdes. I promised Our Lady of Lourdes."

'There's a pub in Heuwagen in Basel and I promised a friend I'd meet him there.

'You can get accommodation in Paddington on the way for £20 a night. Share with someone else.'

He turned to me. 'Are you a Traveller. Do you light fires?'

He asked me where I was from and when I told him he said, 'I stood there with seventeen Connemara ponies once and sold none of them.'

On his fingers rings with horses' heads, saddles, hash plant.

His bumster trousers showed John Galliano briefs.

Two stygian hounds approached the ride followed by an owner with warfare orange hair, in a rainbow hoodie jacket, who called Mack after one of them.

He pulled up his jacket and underlying layers to show a tattoo Makaveli on his butter-mahogany abdomen.

'I got interested in Machiavelli because Tupac was interested in him. Learnt all about him. An Italian philosopher. Nikolo is his first name. Put his tattoo all over my body. Spelt it Makaveli. Called my Rottweiler-Staffordshire terrier cross breed after him. Mack.

'Modge is the long haired black terrier.

'Do you know that Tupac Amaru Shakur was named by his mother after an Inca sentenced to death by the Spaniards?

'In Inca language: Shining Serpent.

'Do you know that when the Florentines were trying to recapture Pisa Machiavelli was begged because he was a philosopher to stay at headquarters but he answered,' and the youth thrust out his chest like Arnold Schwarzenegger for this bit, 'that he must be with his soldiers because he'd die of sadness behind the lines?

'They say Tupac was shot dead in Las Vegas. There was no funeral. He's alive as you or me.

'I'm reading a book about the Kray Twins now.

'Beware of sneak attacks.'

And then he went off with Mack and Modge singing the song Tupac wrote about his mother, 'Dear Mama.'

'When I was a child my father used take me to Ballyheigue every year.

'There's a well there.

'The priest was saying Mass beside it during the Penal Days and the Red Coats turned up with hounds.

'Three wethers jumped from the well, ran towards the sea.

'The hounds chased them, devoured them and were drowned.

'The priest's life was spared.'

They were of Thomond, neither of Munster or Connaught, Thomond bodies, Thomond pectorals.

The other occasion I met Kennedy was on a warm February Saturday.

He was sitting in a Ford Focus on Hyde Road in red silky football shorts with youths in similar attire.

He introduced me to one of them, Razz, who had an arm tattoo of a centurion in a G-string.

'I was in Cloverhill. Remand prison near a courthouse in Dublin. Then Mountjoy. You'd want to see the bleeding place. It was filthy. The warden stuck his head in the cell one day and "You're for Portlaoise." They treat you well in Portlaoise.'

'What were you in jail for?'

'A copper wouldn't ask me that.'

A flank of girls in acid-pink and acid-green tops was hovering near this portmanteau of manhood like coprophagous—dung-eating—gulls hovering near cows for the slugs in their dung.

A little girl in sunglasses with mint green frontal frames, flamingo wings, standing nearby, said to a little girl in a lemon and peach top who was passing:

'There are three birthday cards inside for you, Tiffany.'

'It's not my birthday.'

'It is your fucking birthday.'

And then she began chasing the other like a skua down Hyde Road, in the direction of the bus station, screaming, 'Happy Birthday to you. Happy Birthday to you.'

Flowers of the magnolia come first in Pery Square Park near the Bus Station, tender yellow-green leaf later.

A Traveller boy cycled by the sweet chestnut blossoms of Pery Square Park the day they found Kennedy's body, firing heaped on his handlebars.

I am forced to live in a city of Russian tattooists, murderously shaven heads, Romanian accordionists, the young in pall bearers' clothes—this is the hemlock they've given me to drink.

The Maigue in West Limerick, as I crossed it, was like the old kettles Kennedy's ancestors used mend.

Travellers used make rings from old teaspoons and sometimes I wondered if they could make rings from the discarded Hackenberg lager cans or Mr Sheen All-Surface Polish cans beside the Metal Bridge.

I am living in the city for a year when a man who looks as if his face has been kicked in by a stallion, approaches me on the street.

'I'm from Limerick city and you're from Limerick city. I know a Limerick city face. I haven't seen you there for a while. How many months did you get?'

Basking Adder

We wandered through a field of bulls. Maybe
You thought me seeing you afraid was worse.
You trudged up a hill of briars and gorse
For a dull view I said we had to see.
You listened to me naming the wild flowers
And thought you ought to learn them off by heart
So that their country names would be a part
Of something we could later say was ours.
But you had never seen a snake until that
Adder basking by the path on Golden Cap.
Its scales, like tiny teeth, compressed at the smell
Of our breaths and I, who'd told you that
I kept snakes as a boy, stepped back
As you leaned closer to watch its neck swell.

Stephen Devereux

Teenage Rebel Poem

Hated school.
Hated Math.
Hated Irish.
Hated French.
Hated my scratchy, grey uniform trousers,
the ones my father
bought me after I wore the ends of my old
pair away, letting them drag in the mud,
hating them so much.

My father said:
'You don't know the meaning of the word hate, son.
You couldn't possibly hate all those things.'
Hate was a very strong word, he said.
Son.

So I wrote a message to my father
right where he'd be sure to see it—
high up on the left thigh of my new,
scratchy, grey uniform trousers
the ones he paid twenty-five euro for—
I drew a box on my thigh.
Inside the box I wrote:
'I do not want to live inside a box.'
I wrote it in blue biro.
It shows up better on grey than the red.
And when my father saw it
he didn't say a word about the twenty-five euro.
I had to hand it to him.
That must have cost him a lot more in restraint
than twenty-five euro worth.

Then I dropped out of school
and went to live in New Zealand,
as far outside the box as I could get.

Alyn Fenn

Feast Days

Declan Sweeney

I wanted to sit in the shade and drink beer but Rosa wouldn't have it. We were taking the bus despite her hatred of buses. And it was my fault the car hadn't been fixed. The mechanic was sick I told her. But no. That too was my fault somehow. And we were going to the village come hell or high water. The old people were already queuing. Because that's what they do best, she jeered. Look at them. She made no attempt to keep her voice down. She pushed me forward in front of a small man with a neatly-ironed short-sleeved shirt. She said most of the men looked like they'd come from an ironing competition. I asked her to speak in English at least. She ignored me and continued in Spanish. She stared defiantly at the man's immaculate wife.

People huddled around bags or baskets or boxes. It was more like a market than a bus stop. They argued and shouted. There was a lot of talking about the new administration and the bus fares. Rosa waved me on. Give me the tickets, she said, stepping onto the bus. She had the mobile in her other hand. She rang her mother to say she would have to pick us up when she came down for the milk. The driver checked our tickets and called her guapa. He didn't disguise his lechery but I let it go.

I was trying to get Rosa seated when the fat woman got on. She came sideways past the driver. From the middle of the bus, even through the din, you could pick out the sound of her gasping. The driver had shouted about the door closing as she came laboriously up the steps. She came down the aisle complaining loudly about the driver. The driver complained about latecomers mucking up the schedule for everybody. Rosa could tell he was a socialist. The fat woman, like the rest of these bloody villagers, is a fascist. I hoped she wasn't going to start about Franco. Those fascists, she explained, think they can hold everyone to ransom. Franco is dead, she said loudly. I asked her to pass me the water. That driver has his job to do, she added. I took the aisle seat. The fat woman brushed against me. Her perfume intoxicated. I was relieved when she kept moving. She didn't stop complaining about her arm getting caught in the door, and there was a litany of officials who would be receiving a full account. An old man near the back was visibly impressed by several names mentioned and nodded continually in her direction. When the driver pulled away and turned the radio on the teenagers applauded.

The village was about an hour from the city and it was the first stop. We came along the valley close to the stream and the quilted alfalfa. The parched slopes rose on either side. Already, at noon, the heat was establishing a firm grip. People were mopping their brows, conversation became subdued. One woman fumbled with her beads. I leant forward so Rosa wouldn't see her and initiate a commentary. I put my face close to hers and we looked across the treetops, waiting for the point where the river would make its reappearance, always, though I'd often made this journey, with the hint of surprise. Once the river returned you could look up to the distant spire and count the twists and turns to the village perimeter.

When the bus stopped and the doors opened we could hear the band practise way above on the square. The salsa sounds got everyone talking and moving. The driver, pulling his sunglasses down, swung out of the bus. He greeted the woman coming out of the bar onto the patio. She wore a white blouse and a dark skirt. Her long black hair was tied up. She swung a bar towel in the air and took several provocative turns on the patio, amongst the tables. A wonderful smell of fish and herbs came from the bar. The savour of charcoal. The driver gave the towel a twirl. The waitress evaded him deftly. Someone on the bus made a comment and there was a lot of laughter. I watched Rosa on the step of the bus, unperturbed, looking towards the hills. She exuded a regal indifference. She waited for me to help her down. We took the bag and the cardboard box from the hold. The waitress cracked the bar towel like a whip and went back into the bar followed by two of the passengers. The doors closed and the bus sunk away from them, with a blast of exhaust fumes and a smell of diesel, into the belly of the hill.

I was still gasping for a beer but Rosa said we should wait. I shrugged. An old woman with a stiff perm came out of the bar and stared at us. It made me uneasy. I always complained about the way people stared. It made Rosa laugh. If someone stared at Rosa she was all the more likely to do something outrageous. She took a few steps in the woman's direction and looked past her to the farmhouse north of the village where smoke curled through the still air. That's where they are making the giant paella, she said. A few weeks before she had shown me the large pan that spanned the width of a truck. The woman with the perm backed away. She sat on a stool looking defeated and turned her back to us.

Rosa picked up the cardboard box and crossed the road to the bus shelter. I followed her and placed my bag on the seat. From that side we had a better view of the mountain track to her mother's place. She scanned the roads that etched the side of the mountain and connected all the new houses in bands. There was very little movement, and people round their houses were obscured by trees or walls, or simply distance. After a little concentration I could pick out the white dot of her mother's house. I followed the line of the road to the inevitable dust cloud, the black object that could have been a cockroach, quivering in the heat. Rosa had already spotted the jeep. She was looking at her watch. She's coming down for the milk, she said.

Teresa was far too small for the Russian jeep and she made it look like a tank. Rosa declared that she drove it like a tank. Mama, she gasped, when the jeep lurched onto the pavement thirty yards away. Shouting was often their way. Teresa was shouting back before she even got out of the jeep. She got entangled in the seatbelt, though she never wore it properly. It could choke you, she said. She cursed the Russians, her bronzed head barely visible, like a classical bust on the dashboard. Without ceremony she climbed out and bustled around to the back. Rosa and I strained to kiss her on the cheek. She carried on talking about one thing or another. A description or a complaint would remain unfinished because some other thing crossed her mind. She might return to it later in the middle of something else. It was a feature that Rosa shared, one that made communication difficult, and shouting necessary. So it seemed.

Teresa took the milk containers and crossed to the bar, still talking loudly. Rosa followed her to the door, shouting within, oblivious of the two couples at the table and the woman with the perm who looked more defeated. My tongue was hanging out. I had to use my sleeve to mop my brow. I heard Manolo's name bandied back and forth. That was the gist of her agitation. Manolo the jack-of-all-trades had delayed her with his woes. The stories of his wayward wife which always roused my suspicion. The way he confided in Teresa, insinuating. Always saying too much, looking for that sympathetic shoulder. If it wasn't his wife it was some battle with the mayor of the village, guaranteed to get her onside, because Teresa, he knew, had her own battles with the mayor. She was likely to launch into one of her tirades about the fascists.

She came out to me bursting. She put the milk on the table much to the old couple's dismay. You know what that bastard did, she was telling me. Even she realised that her tirade would have to be tempered in that bar. They were friends with the mayor. Unable to contain herself she came to me, to unburden. I wasn't sure which bastard but I didn't interrupt. I was accustomed to picking up these threads at random. I had given up any expectation of things being evident. Things would crop up in conversation that would illuminate something whispered days before. I leant forward encouragingly. Rosa sighed. Let's have a beer, I suggested and walked into the bar. Teresa had to have her say so she followed bottling it up as best she could until we stood at the end of the counter near the empty tables. Most of the customers were parked up the other end near the drinks fridge and the jukebox, apart from four sour-looking men in their twenties. They were at the corner table. I thought they were from another village because the locals only sat at the tables if they were eating. One of them looked at Rosa as if he knew her but didn't say anything. I stared at him for a second but Teresa had my elbow and started talking again. I ordered three beers.

She was unrelenting with her story. I had heard it before. How the mayor and his family had cheated her over a piece of land. Rosa knew how to derail her. She asked if the animals had been fed, and Teresa was back again complaining about being delayed by Manolo. Her whole day would be thrown into disarray. She couldn't even finish her beer. I picked up the baggage, as I always did, and placed it carefully in the back of the jeep, knowing that one or both of the women would come and rearrange what I had done. I was determined not to be put out. The men at the table were watching us leave. Rosa studiously ignored them. The woman with the perm walked up the steep incline towards the square with a pig's leg on her shoulder. I looked at the black feet in her scrawny grip. Teresa was moving the bag round like a sleepwalker. That woman was so fat, Rosa said suddenly. Both of us looked at her and climbed into the jeep. Teresa had no idea she meant the woman on the bus. It was another way for Rosa to distract her mother. That's how they carried on.

The jeep bounced around on the stony road. Teresa found it very hard to find the right speed, and when she did she couldn't maintain it, couldn't stop herself jerking the accelerator. She was fretting about the chickpeas and the cod that she had soaked overnight and cooked that morning with the spinach. I told Tanya to lift the pot, she moaned. Rosa bit her tongue for once. We both knew that Teresa never let her mother near the kitchen for some reason. All the women in the family were great cooks but fought like hell when it came to the details. Her voice began to soar again when she described Tanya trying to add a little extra paprika to the dish. She looked at me. I shook my head. Rosa put her arms round my neck and pointed to the Alsatian at the gate. Tito, the three of us exclaimed in unison, and broke up laughing as the dog started to bark.

Rosa's grandmother observed us from the balcony. Come away, Tito, she shouted unconvincingly, and the dog ignored her. Tanya made no attempt to move. She never moved suddenly, not because she was old, but she was groomed at odds with the bustle of her family. There was always an air of preservation about her, a faded hard-bitten grandeur. Her skin too was lighter in tone. She was proud of her peachy skin. She came from a family of wealthy landowners in Segovia and paler skin, she once told me, conveyed status. It meant you didn't work the sun-baked fields. When her father lost everything through gambling she became a seamstress and never forgave him. She waved like a queen as I opened the gate and struggled with the dog. She went back inside before Teresa found something to shout about. I knew she would be sitting in her corner, bracing herself, taking her tablets.

One day that dog will break some bones, I said. No one listened. I stood at the bottom of the stone stairs and let them fall through the door with the dog herding them. All three talking at once and the dog barking. Tanya had moved to the sink to give herself an air of usefulness. She had picked up an old cloth from beneath the sink, clutching at it, with no real idea what she was going to do. Teresa grabbed the cloth and put it back in its place, going straight to check the pots like someone who'd been burgled. You've been eating again, Rosa taunted her grandmother, and the old woman flapped despite all her resolve. I walked over and kissed her on both cheeks. I was surprised by her soft and perfumed skin.

She was relieved at my intervention, and took the opportunity to get back to her seat in the corner, the safest place in the room.

Rosa thrust one of the milk containers at me. I pretended for a moment that I didn't know what to do with it but she paid no attention. I did what I usually did and took it down the backstairs to the storeroom below. I put it in the second fridge beside the long freezer. The outer wall of the basement was made of glass doors that folded open on days like these. A series of broad terraces composed the slope towards the boundary saplings. The coops and chicken huts filled the bottom terrace. Vegetable drills occupied the one above. A series of flat stones formed steps from one terrace to the next. The chickens were agitated and brought the dog to investigate, but he came tearing towards me when I lit a cigarette. He waited for me to throw something but I managed to get him to sit quiet. I liked to look down over the valley. It still gave me a sense of well-being every time and I wondered if the others felt the same, or maybe it wore off. I could see the church in the tree-lined village square. The village was carved like a conch on the lower slopes beyond the river and the road, a few people scattered like ants. The village stage was like a matchbox. This evening, in the shade, the place would swarm and the band would echo all the way up here. The matchbox would shake. I tracked the sky for any sign of the eagles. They soared as a pair. But there was nothing, not a speck on the endless bright canvas.

Teresa called out to Rosa. I could hear her ask Rosa to remind me to bring up the firewood. I shouted back before Rosa had time to say anything. There was some comment from Tanya and laughter above. At the sound of their voices the dog got excited again and I couldn't persuade him to sit. Ye have this dog ruined, I shouted, but they ignored me. I resisted shouting again. I came from a family of whisperers, Rosa told me. Even the trees used to whisper around the old family house. It was an uneven, windswept place in the Shannon basin, sprawling out from the original grey render, a room extended to one side, then another out the back towards disintegrating sheds. It was an outworn, sacrificial place, and my brother couldn't understand why I sold it only a year after my father died. He could only see it as a betrayal, and not the escape from an inevitable extirpation. For a second I imagined my brother standing beside me, only for a second, because I knew he never would.

The dog scrambled for the gate. He gave it a ferocious rattle. Someone, not yet visible, must be walking up the road, or maybe one of the hunters was crossing the field. I put the cigarette out and dropped the butt under a stone. I half expected to hear Rosa tell me not to do that. I gathered some logs and went upstairs. The smells of food and spices were everywhere. The women moved around like jugglers. Rosa chopped the garlic into thin slices and mixed it with the parsley. Teresa lifted the pan of sliced potatoes from the flame so her daughter could sprinkle the garlic. Tanya beat the egg mixture in a bowl. The pot with cod and chickpeas was on a low heat. Teresa took the egg mixture from her mother and added a dash of milk, beating it to her own taste. Rosa passed me a bottle of Valdepeñas to open. I popped the cork and Teresa was adamant about keeping it for the cod. The other two complained. Rosa passed around some sherry. She insisted I try it. Then she took me by the hand to the balcony as if she had timed it to perfection. Look, she pointed with the sherry glass. The sunlight sparkled on the glass. Two small specks oscillated between the peaks. The eagles appeared.

From the highest point, against the sun, they eased from the face of the mountain, and floated down through the valley, riding invisible currents from one side to another, passing way above the house where they held for an instant, before dipping to the lowest point near the river, scaling a hill on the other side. They continued the length of the valley until they became specks again, and vanished.

Teresa shouted to shut the door and keep the dog out. We remained for a second staring at the emptiness where the eagles had been, savouring the elation. Teresa placed the chunks of bread beside the plate of red peppers arranged in a star. She drizzled oil over the peppers. She added crispy bacon to the wild mushrooms and beckoned everyone to the table. Rosa took small beers from the freezer. Teresa refused one. She flicked the heads off two of them and gave one to me. Teresa smiled when she placed the tortilla in front of me. The pot with the cod and chickpeas was placed in the centre of the table. When we were all seated Teresa waited for me to pour her some wine. Tanya sipped her iced water like a martyr. I looked at Rosa. She had her eyes closed briefly. I knew she was thinking of the eagles. There was still a sense of flight and mystery in the pit of the stomach. You're not saying grace, Teresa said disparagingly. She had no truck with religion or its remotest trappings. No, Mama, Rosa snapped, and started putting salad on the plates. Only a little for me, Tanya said meekly, like a stranger in the house. Only a little, Rosa scoffed, putting a large portion on the old woman's plate. I poured her a tot of wine. Her lips puckered, the smallest of protests.

You're lucky to have a grandmother, I told Rosa. Everyone has one, she said. Alive I mean. Sometimes it was hard to tell if she was serious or what she was thinking. She had a way of disappearing suddenly, before your eyes, and someone I didn't recognise took her place. That was always a scary moment. Like a recurring dream I had where she walked through a doorway and didn't come back. That thought left an aftertaste. If she wasn't herself, if one day she didn't return, then I would no longer be able to sit at this table, amongst these people. I, too, would disappear.

When Tanya had cleared her plate, and the others had long finished, she reached for another chunk of bread. No bread, Teresa barked. No more bread, Rosa chimed. I resisted defending the old lady. It would serve no purpose, change nothing. Tanya clicked her tongue and put the bread back. Rosa always said it was an insult to the cook to eat bread after your meal. She took the remainder of the bread from the table and placed it on the sideboard under a cloth. Teresa began making coffee. The dog barked and rattled the main gate. I saw Rosa glance at the clock. Rosa didn't look out the window like Teresa did. Instead, she moved to the door like someone expecting a visitor. We could all see the man coming up the hill towards the gate. Teresa recognised him before I did. One of the sour young men from the bar. She became very agitated and spoke too quickly for me to understand. It brought Tanya to her feet. Those drug dealers should be run out of the village, Tanya said. Both women looked accusingly at Rosa, but she went quickly down the steps, out of view. I felt an irrational fear when I couldn't see her anymore, like the feeling of loss I had in the dream, a dread of old ways.

I ran down the steps, past Rosa, towards the gate, shouting. I couldn't get past the dog quickly enough. I cursed the man as he turned back and I struggled to hold the dog. I almost let him loose but I was distracted by a line of people with flags and banners, moving along the bank of the river. From a distance it looked like parts of the riverbank were slowly shifting. People were banging drums. I dragged the dog back and went inside.

The women upstairs hadn't moved. Teresa sipped her coffee. Tanya wiped her hands with a napkin. She didn't look at me for several seconds, but when she did there was a faint smile, a kind of acknowledgement. Teresa poured calvados into two small handcrafted tumblers, quirky shapes. She offered me one.

Through the balcony window I could see Rosa down by the pool. The anxiety circled, like the dream when I watched her going through the door, not knowing if she would return. Her head was tilted upwards, undeterred, scanning the heights of the valley. I savoured the calvados, its bite and its heat, the rawness dissolving into warmth. It was like an invisible hand soothing my body, touching my eyes so I could see those distant specks again, the eagles spiralling closer.

I could see them come towards her through the valley. She lifted her head, without turning, aware of me approaching. I put my arms round her as they flew overhead. I smelled her skin, and that wild mix of pine and verbena blown up from the river. We both inhaled. It's like lemons, she said.

Hide and Seek

Into the woods we follow the clues
you planted in my sleep:

your scarf hangs on a bush, a note
in your unmistakable hand, illegible

to the child's eye. In the pockets
of your discarded coat, newspaper

clippings, cartoons to make us laugh,
stories that carry a message for each of us

between the lines. The damp print
blackens my fingers. I almost chant out loud

What time is it Mister Wolf?
wait for the thrill as you pounce

from behind a tree, snarling
It's six o'clock and it's my supper-time,

your hair still dark as you loom over
three white-socked, squealing girls.

Instead, silence drips from the wet leaves,
like fear. We will not find you here, today.

I will come back alone, follow the paths
of walks we shared, and where the trees

start to thin, I will hear your voice,
still waiting to be found.

Lorna Shaughnessy

The Waking of Eimear Kinnane

Deirdre Gleeson

Once there was a man who was unhappy. His wife was dead, her body was lost in the sea. But that was not the reason why Malachy Kinnane was unhappy.

He sat at the head of the table in his kitchen watching the dead logs in the fire collapsing in on themselves. The chair to his left was empty. He had asked Rose Hanlon to sit there, but she had refused. They had all refused.

The table was sweating with the wings and legs of roasted birds, and the wheels of bread that Rose and Nellie Hayes had brought; Tommy Larkin and Johnnie Malone had come with bottles of wine and of whiskey. Malachy would be eating for a week as soon as he could get them out of his house.

The eyes of his guests swung back to that empty chair like the tongue that returns to a hole where a tooth had been. But they were looking at him too. No doubt of that.

He felt the prickle of them on his skin. Their eyes on him. Seeing how he was taking it. His gestures were measured. The drop of his head. The slump of his shoulders when he thought no one was looking. Was he drinking too much? Was he drinking enough?

They would offer their sly kindnesses. Nellie Hayes would go through Eimear's things if he was too upset. Rose Hanlon would bring food over and check the contents of the presses while she was at it.

And the talk? The hissing whispers after Mass. In the shop. Over tea. After a pint or two. Relentless. Spawning other stories, in other places, over other drinks, with the glance around and the lean in.

Nellie Hayes was still watching the empty chair when she started telling the story about the time Eimear came down to the shop, with blood on her face.

'I told you before—Eimear fell going down the hill on the ice,' Malachy said.

Nellie shrugged, 'But imagine, she didn't pay any heed to the blood pouring out the top of her head? She was some woman.'

Malachy shivered. They were remaking the dead. As always. Knitting the flesh of words back on their bones. The coward would be wise, the angry man an idealist, and so on. Recast from finer stuff, in an endless stream of stories that comforted the living. When they died, they too would be remembered and remade.

Malachy never liked it. Let them be. Do not call the dead from the ground.

He shivered again. It had crept in with the wind under the door. The smell of her. Fingering him, trailing around him. He sniffed the air, trying to find the stink of her, from her dress on the side table, the cushion from the chair she had sat on.

The wind was rattling the slates on the roof.

His guests had stopped speaking. Tommy Larkin scraped his blade against the knuckle of his tobacco. Johnnie Malone's shadow twisted and pawed at the wall as his hand reached towards the bottle for another fill of his glass.

Tommy Larkin said, 'Eimear was a lovely quiet girl all the same.'

Malachy heard the hail of her fingers on the windowpane.

'It's only the branches of the oak tree on the glass,' Rose said.

The clawing of the branches against Malachy's heart made him shake. He drummed his fingers ever faster on the table.

'Jesus, Malachy, will you quit it? You're scaring the life out of us,' Johnnie Malone laughed. He pulled his chair closer to the fire.

Nellie Hayes was telling about Eimear and Batt Lowry one time after Mass. Batt had been pushing this story on everyone about his uncle George who died in Canada. But Eimear had just looked at him, and said nothing. Finally Batt had run out of juice and left the church grounds altogether. No one had ever stopped Batt in his tracks.

'She was a lovely quiet girl,' Tommy Larkin said, sucking wetly on his pipe. Malachy shuddered.

He saw the roundness of her face at the window.

'It's only the harvest moon rising,' Rose said, but she pulled the beads out of her bag.

Eimear Kinnane was so cold. She was hunkered down by the hen coop at the side of the house, peering around at the door.

She thought Malachy would be alone. But by the time she reached the house, they were already arriving. Bringing him gifts. So she waited. Watching the dance of orange light from the window.

She would walk to warm herself.

She would go in.

She settled back against the wall, pulling the thin cloth of her borrowed dress around her. The wind had picked up again.

Malachy's moon was so large, fevering in his head.

'She was a lovely quiet girl all the same,' Tommy said.

Malachy heard a bird dying in the yard.

*

Deirdre Gleeson

The hens were loud. Maybe Malachy hadn't fed them. Maybe they knew the smell of her. Eimear kicked the wire behind her with her heel. Their round squawking filled her ears. Someone would hear.

She kicked the coop again. The birds were smashing their wings against the wire. Turning the wooden handle, she lifted the sagging end of the gate so it did not scrape against the gravel. With one eye on the door she shooed the hens out of the coop. Let Rose Hanlon or Nellie Hayes bring Malachy his eggs in the morning. She smiled at that.

She felt the downy head of one of the chicks brush against her ankle like a kiss. None of them had left—they were waiting for food. A tiny beak nipped her bare foot. Their noise grew louder.

Someone would hear.

She reached down and picked up a chick, more fluff than flesh, the bones of its leg tiny in her fist. Her eyes never left the door. She held the body close and warm in one hand. Its head lay soft in her other. She turned it. Gently. Gently as the world turns or an idea turns—in and around on itself. Until her hands separated and she held the chick's head in one palm and its heart in another. It was easy. She laid them both on the ground beside her, and took another chick. They were so loud.

She did not hold them gently now. She turned her back from the door. Reached for them. One, two at a time. Crushing them in her fist. Wrenching each head from the body.

Then the frenzy of it left her, and she breathed easy again. She stood in the yard, oblivious to the coldness of the wind now, staring down the slope of Malachy's fields to the sea.

The moon was a blade on the water.

Malachy opened the front door and stepped out into the yard.

Eimear stood before him with blood and feathers on her hands. His thoughts thrashed about in his head. She's-dead, she's-not-dead. She's-dead-not-dead.

I'm dreaming, he thought. His teeth clattered. Nellie Hayes and the rest of them had raised his wife's ghost from the dead with their words.

Then the crowd was standing behind him in the yard, beside him, in front, moving towards her. Eimear did not stop looking at him. She wiped her fingers off a dress that Malachy did not recognise.

Their voices swarmed around her. Hands touched her shoulders, her head, her arms. She was a fruit picked apart by birds. Her eyes never left his face.

'For God's sake, bring the poor woman inside!' Nellie Hayes said.

With the light on her, they all fell back a bit. It was Eimear all right, but she seemed a little bit leaner, her hair a shade darker, the curve in her jaw a little sharper, her nails a shade longer. The more they looked, the more unreal she seemed to them. As if they had never seen her before. But they knew it was her, they knew it was Eimear.

She saw the table sagging with food and drink, the lit fire and abandoned glasses and, although Tommy Larkin stood in front to block her view, Eimear saw too the narrow table by the door with her own white dress laid out on it. She walked past him, towards the table. The dress lay flat, the arms folded across each other on the lap. She ran her finger along a lace sleeve. Eimear looked at the lifeless dress on the table and she wondered for a minute if they were right.

If she was dead.

If she was visiting her house for one last time, before she passed on to the other side.

She felt like crying for the part of Eimear Kinnane that lay dead inside that dress on the table. But she felt too the cold creep from the flagstones up her scratched and tired legs. And the ache in her back. And the fury in her. So she did not weep.

'It's bad luck to wake the living,' Johnnie Malone said to his glass.

'What happened to you, Eimear?' Nellie Hayes said.

Eimear felt hot. They were looking at her. She felt like her tongue was too big for her mouth.

'What did you think happened?' her throat was closing in on itself.

Their faces were bright, puzzled.

'We thought you had fallen,' Tommy Larkin said.

'Thought you were out walking,' said Rose Hanlon.

They looked at Malachy, like children.

'You were tired,' Malachy said.

The neighbours looked at each other. Tired was a good word. Malachy's arms twined around Eimear, pulling her into him. Smothering her body in his. He pushed out dry kisses on the top of her head.

'So was that what happened?' Nellie Hayes asked.

Eimear felt the swarm of their eyes on her skin. They were touching her, handling her with the carefulness of their words. But Nellie could never control herself. She was dropping glances at Rose. She made herself smile at them.

'I don't remember,' Eimear said.

'I must have been walking,' she said.

'I must have been tired,' she said.

Nellie nodded. She rubbed Eimear's shoulder. Smiled. Exchanged another look with Rose. Eimear felt the rod of Malachy's arm against her back.

She didn't think she could look at him, but she did. She forced herself to look at him, as if she'd never seen him before. As if she was tired. As if she had been walking. As if she had not been waiting outside of her house for the last hours.

'But you should rest now,' Malachy said. His fingers snaked around her own.

The crowd sighed. Disappointed. The night was cut short. But it was not every night that a woman came back from the dead, and there would be plenty of time for talking on the way back down to the village.

She could not have him touching her any more. Eimear's tongue was enormous in her mouth, and strange to her, as if it had never known how to move or to say a word. It was important that she say a word.

Eimear reached for Nellie Hayes. Took the older woman's hand.

'If we cannot have a wake,' she said, 'let us have a party.' Her lips were sticking together. She was hot. She felt Malachy's eyes burning on her, but she did not look at him.

'Hear, hear!' Johnnie raised his half-empty glass to her and drained it.

'I am a little tired though,' Eimear said, 'I would like to sit.'

Tommy Larkin gestured to the seat beside Malachy's. 'Sit down here in your own chair.' She smiled at Tommy but sat instead in Malachy's seat at the head of the table.

Malachy wedged himself into the smaller chair beside her.

'Husband,' Eimear said, and Malachy felt her voice vibrate through him, pushing in the cavity of his chest. 'I am hungry. Will you give me the goosemeat on your plate?'

Malachy felt the eyes of the others on him as he gave his plate to her. He watched as she took his knife with the bone handle and put the point of it into the flesh of the goose, slicing the meat and the sinew away from the bone. She left the knife back on the table, and she took the meat in her fingers. She ate the skin and the flesh and the fat. She sucked the meat left on each bone slowly and dropped it on the floor when she was done.

'Will you fetch me another plate?' she asked.

Malachy piled again his plate with meat and returned it to her. So it went until a ring of bones on the floor circled her chair and her chin glistened with the grease of the goose she had eaten.

'I'd like to tell a story,' Eimear said.

Rose smiled and loosened her grip on her beads. Tommy's black nails happily worked his tobacco into the bowl of his pipe. Johnnie poured himself another drink.

'Let's be having you then, girlie,' Tommy said, and he leaned back on his chair.

'Once there was a man who was unhappy,' Eimear said. 'Every morning he took his father's boat out and went fishing. Every day he drilled seaweed into the grey soil his father had passed down to him. He nursed his sick lambs. He pulled his sheep out of the ditches in his fields. Every night before he went home to his wife, he watched those fields gleaming black in the moonlight and he wished from his deepest heart for a son.

'The routine of his life used to comfort him. The living. The dying. The trees bursting with fruit. Their shiver in winter. Now his apples rotted and festered in the grass.

'But the seasons passed and his wife gave him not son nor daughter. Without a son to pass his farm to, what was the point in the endless ploughing, and pulling, the shearing and seeding?

'Each spring was now an enemy. Each spring became another to be endured. Another start of another growth. But he and his wife getting older with each flowering, each ripening, each falling, each dying.

'Every night he carried his disappointment back to his wife who waited for him at the window. She would lie beneath him, as he emptied himself into her. She would feel the weight of his farm on her. Feel the press of the soil between his shoulder blades. Until it seemed to her that he did not walk on the soil, but already lay under it. Under the weight of it.

'She would rise after, as he lay slumped, blind in his sleep. And she would look at the moon. She would pick at the tightness of the skin on her belly, as she watched the swell of the moon. She would pick and pick at herself, until the skin burned under her nails as she looked at the moon that grew fat when she did not. She hated the fatness of the moon.

'She told herself she would conceive. But each month the moon grew large, and then her blood came. She came to hate the blood and the flesh that had failed her. The belly that would not carry her child. The breasts that would not feed her child. The arms that would not hold her child. She hated the flesh that could not make her child.

'She ate less. She smiled less. She cried less now. Her tears had turned to salt in her sockets.

'Then one night as she looked at the moon and she picked at the flesh on her arm, a flake of her skin came off in her hand. Transparent as the moonlight. Floating slow past her to the floor.

'At her second touch, another layer of skin fell from her. Half the length of her arm and falling away from her like the wing from a giant grey butterfly. Shiny and clear and collapsing to dust as the air ran through it.

'The more she rubbed, layer after layer fell away. Sheaves of her skin, falling soft and silent as snow. Spilling into dust at her feet.

'She could not stop scratching herself. Flakes of her fell away as she walked. When she lifted an arm. Turned her head. As the back of her leg touched the hem of her dress. She grew used to the fine coat of dust that trailed behind her wherever she went in the house. But still she looked at the moon, and still she picked at herself.

'So the woman became more flake than flesh, slowly turning to dust. The ashes of her sadness lay on her husband's pillow and covered his bread and seeped into him as he slept at night.'

'And the husband?' Johnnie Larkin asked. 'What happened to him then?' He laughed and winked at Malachy.

Rose was leaning away from Eimear. Her hand was in her pocket, clamping her beads. But Nellie was watching Eimear, her head tilted, looking at the strain and flush on the younger woman's face as if she'd never seen it before, listening to the catch in her breath as she sank back into the chair.

'I'm sure that they all lived happily ever after,' Malachy said. He filled the glasses of his guests.

'Or they made each other miserable to their dying day. Isn't that the way these things usually go?' he laughed. 'I had never guessed that my wife was such a storyteller.'

His hand clasped her shoulder. Eimear pulled her body away from him. She looked tired. She looked as if her body would not hold her head except for the wooden backbone of the chair.

Malachy smiled at her and at the crowd.

'I think we might call it a night,' Malachy said.

The round rap of a hand on the door interrupted him. The Widow Mullen came into the room.

'I'm sorry I'm late.'

She saw Eimear collapsed in the chair at the head of the table and stepped back against the door. Malachy went to her and he led her to a seat. They gave her a drink. Malachy watched the wet lip of the glass against her mouth.

Eimear roused herself. Did the others not see the drag of the buttons on Maeve Mullen's new coat? Or the recent roundness to her face?

Eimear said, 'Husband, I am thirsty too. Will you give me a drink from your glass?'

Malachy waited. They were watching him. He passed her his drink. She drained the glass and held it back out to him.

'Will you pour me another?' she said. He did as she asked, holding the bottle in both hands, but still the wine sloshed out, clotting in pools at the base of the glass, staining the wood of the table, his hands.

Eimear drank from her husband's wine until his bottles were empty, and her teeth and her tongue were black from it, but she did not grow merry from it, and neither did her thirst diminish.

'Johnnie, my story is not done yet,' Eimear said, 'I will tell the rest of it now.'

'Once there was a man who was unhappy,' Eimear said. 'He lived in a house that was cold. Even when he lay in his bed in the dark, when sleep should curl snug around him, he felt colder than the stars hanging in the sky on a clear night. The cold bit into his skin, and began to eat the flesh from his bones and freeze the blood inside him.

'When he looked at his wife, he grew colder. He could not touch her, be near her. So he circled her, small circles at first, the other side of the bed, the table, the room, then the house. The far side of the garden. The morning in the currach, the evening in the field.

'He took to walking. The force of her pushing him out the door, up the yard, out on to the path towards the black woods at the foot of the mountains. As the days went by his walks grew longer and wider, but the coldness in him would not shift, even when he walked far up the hill, beyond the fields behind his house, up to where the trees began and he could no longer see his cold roof and the cold walls of his house.

'One afternoon on his walk, he met a woman leaning against the wall. He knew of her. Her husband had died two days after they wed. He had drowned out fishing. They said she was bad luck. But a man who lives in a cold house does not think much about luck. The young widow had a jug in her hand.

'The widow said she thought he might like something to drink. He could see the jug was brimming with water and a little of it had spilled on the dry earth in front of her, and even on her skirt. As she offered the jug to him his fingers touched her hand. It was soft and warm. He felt a shock on his skin. His fingers were swollen and sticky. He felt a stirring in him. And he wondered about the softness of her arms, and her breasts. His face flamed and he drank more water but he did not dare look at her again.

'He hastened away up the path towards the woods.

'She called goodbye to him, laughing. He did not turn back to her. But he thought again about the heat of her hand touching his, before he walked through the pine trees into the darkness of the woods.

'The next day she was waiting again with a jug of water. And she held onto it with her two hands as he took the jug, though it was no heavier than the day before and it did not take two of them to lift it to his lips. So he clasped the jug, curling his hands around her fingers and they lifted it together to his mouth. The water streamed out of it and down his chin and neck and shoulders. And they laughed together, but the heart was thumping in his chest and he felt a heat in him that the water did not cool.

'On the third day, she said the jug was broken, but there was a well at the back of her house if he wanted water and she would show him the way. He felt a pounding in him as she took him by the hand up a path behind her house. At the well he took her shoulders and turned her around and pulled her to him.

'So they were fast together, fixed like a man and his shadow. The man spent every minute he could with the widow woman, except the times when he went back to his cold house. But he found that he did not mind the cold so much any more.

'When the man came back to his wife, he seemed strange to her. He shimmered with heat. The light from him blinded her. She grew clumsy around him.

'His hard brightness shook the walls, rattling the glasses in shelves. Until she dared not look directly at his light. Dared not stand in the same room, for fear of his burning.

'But then he would leave again, and the walls would shiver and fold in on themselves, leaving his wife in the quietness and the coldness and the darkness.'

Johnnie nudged Malachy in the ribs, nearly falling from his chair as he did so.

'Ho ho, Malachy! We didn't think you had it in you!' Johnnie said. His leery gaze flicked over the widow.

A red stain flushed the widow's chest and neck. Malachy grabbed Eimear's wrist, pressing his fingers into her flesh.

'You're hurting me, Malachy,' Eimear said.

He dropped his hand.

'Enough, Eimear! Your words have been true enough and lie enough to cause harm to people in this room,' Malachy said, pointing at the widow.

'Did you not do the same to me with your half-truths?' Eimear said. But she did not stand, and she did not have the heat in her voice that Malachy had.

Tommy Larkin put his hand on Malachy's arm and said: 'Don't mind Johnnie, he's just drunk and he's stirring the pot. It's only a story she's telling.'

'Yes, let her tell her story,' Nellie said, 'for I don't think it's done yet.'

Malachy looked at them all, but they stared back at him. And none of them moved. 'Let's hear her story,' they said. And there was nothing for it, but for Malachy to sit back down in his chair, and to wait for Eimear to speak.

The bottle made a popping sound as Johnnie took another dose, and he said, 'Eimear, have you a story about a woman who walks off the edge of a cliff?'

'Jesus! Johnnie…' Tommy said, dropping his pipe.

'I only know the story of a woman put in a cave,' Eimear said, as she looked at Malachy.

Malachy sat with his eyes closed. He did not see Eimear looking at him, or the eyes of the others on him. He did not move, he waited only for the shape and the spike of her words.

'Once there was a man who was unhappy,' Eimear said. 'He had two women: a small one and a big one, and the big one was growing larger every day. Soon there was not space in his head for the two of them and he knew no rest in the bed of either.

'When the man realised that he wanted a son more than he wanted a wife, he went to the bed of his wife in the middle of the night, and he tied her in a white sheet so that she could not move. He put a strip of the sheet in her mouth so that she could not scream. Then he sat with her in their bedroom, with the tears running down his face and he waited for the moon to dim in the belly of night cloud.

'She was a small woman, and he carried her in his two hands like a bride through the night.

'She thought, he is carrying me to the sea. She thought, he is my husband, he loves me. She thought, he is carrying me to the sea.

'His feet knew the way up the high road behind the houses, along by the hanging fields, and down the other side where the headland dips, where the land is more stone than soil. Where the sea whips the rock. Where the caves are.'

'You know the caves on the beach by the Lady's Steps?' Eimear said. 'They cut back into the rock, go way back. You know when the tide comes in?'

'Go on, go on,' they said.

'From his arms she saw the black loom of cliffs breaking the sky. The stars spun around her as he made his way across the stony beach, grunting as the water splattered his shoes. She heard the smash of the waves breaking their backs again and again on the beach.

'He stepped into the largest cave. Streams of water were already shooting across the floor. The crash of the waves grew softer as he carried her further inside. He would not leave her in the mouth of the cave, where her body would fly out with the sea and the fishermen would find her on the bloody rocks in the morning.

'He leant her against a flattened sheet of rock, then stood back and looked at her. As if he would say something. As if she would say something. He put his lips on her swollen mouth pressing the cloth further down her throat. Then he left.

'She heard the clatter of his feet on the stones as he ran across the beach. Then only the muffle of the sea outside.

'Her bare feet curled with the cold and damp of the rock. Through the mouth of the cave, she could see the slit of sky, and the waves breaking, streaked with foam and moonlight. Inside the cave, as the water came in, she could see nothing, as if the sea had already taken her eyes before he took her body.

'She moved further back against the rock wall, feeling the spike of barnacles in her back. She did not see the water, but she felt the icy bite of it as it slid up her shin, then pulled away again.

'Another wave slapped against her, the shock of the cold pushing her backwards against the rock. Then pulled away again, leaving her sodden, weeping, shaking. Bracing herself for the next wave.

'Her mind was thrashing in her head, slapping itself off the inside of her skull like a dying fish.

'The water streamed up her thighs, her hips. Each wave a knife in her. Each wave reminding her that she could feel colder, wetter. Each wave taking a little piece of her living body away with it out of the cave.

'She thought about her dying. About a head covered by the sea. About a cave filled with water and a woman floating and tumbling in it. But as she thought about these things, and her body began to lose itself, surrendering to the water, her mind shook itself free from the woman's body and flew out into the night.

'The woman's mind saw a boat where a dark-haired man was sleeping among his nets. Her mind put a dream into the fisherman's head.

'He had a vision of a woman in a cave dressed in white, with the waves rising up over her body. In this vision she begged him to come to her and rescue her in the largest cave by the Lady's Steps.

'The waves were up to her chest now, and the woman did not know where her body ended and the water began. But her mind spoke to the wind and the sea. So the wind turned cold and whistled. The sea grew rough. A wave splashed up over the side of the boat wetting the leg of the fisherman and woke him from his sleeping. His mind was full of the vision he had dreamed. He put out his oars and he rowed towards the Lady's Steps.

'The fisherman steered his boat into the mouth of the cave and he saw the woman drowning in the water. He blessed himself, for he thought that God had wanted him to save this woman from her dying. He pulled her into his boat, and he gave her his jacket to cover herself.'

'Hold on, Eimear!' Malachy stood. He was hot, angry. He would deny. The others sat stuck in their chairs. They stared at him, as if they had never seen him before. No one smiled or jeered.

It was over.

He felt hunted. The room was closing in on him.

Eimear did not speak. She put her left arm around Malachy's neck and kissed his mouth.

Her lips felt soft. He tasted salt and honey. Her mouth was wet on his. He remembered her lying in the crook of his arm, the heat of her, the shy smile of her, the hollow of her collar bone, of pleasure twisting in on itself. He remembered his father, his mother's smile, the first sunrise, the thrum of the heat of the sun on a summer day, the painful hollow in him when he kissed her. He was turning inside out.

Malachy felt the sorrow spike in him—he knew he would never feel these things again.

The crowd was standing now, looking to Eimear. Waiting for her to finish it.

The knife with the bone handle found her hand. Twisting her fingers around itself, pressing its cold shape onto her flesh. Her right arm was high behind her, falling like a song, and Eimear Kinnane took the heart of her husband back to her.

Concealment

In the city too
watching things themselves
is to repair our broken knowledge.

At the bus stop a kestrel
scatters sparrows
and there is sky above the traffic.

To this place of reluctance
departing birds come.
A fox steals from a bin.

There is a shore of broken glass
beneath the swings.
We live
in the space between the buildings.

Joseph Horgan

Ye Dancer

Lynsey May

She wis a dancer. Not a stripper like, or one of those girls you'd have got on *Top of The Pops* or that, but a dancer dancer. The kind you wouldnae think you'd ever actually meet. Not like I ever should've met her; but it wis halfway through the festival and I found her and her dancer mates skeltering all over Whistle Binkies, prancing around like it wis some kinda nightclub or something. They wis all high voices and weird clothes but that's not unusual in the summer, you ken.

Anyway, me and Oli had been at some comedy thing down the Pleasance—proper balls it wis—so we'd boosted off for booze that wisnae at festival prices and wis sitting spraffing shite, like you do. Tae listen tae us, you'd think we could've done better than those poor sods. Sods we'd paid guid money to see like. I mean, what kinda funny man are you if you cannae handle a wee bit of heckling? Wish someone had took the mike off of them so we hadnae had tae listen to their 'we're tae guid for this place, but we're gonna take the piss out ourselves tae make it like we dinnae think that' bullshit. We wis a bit riled up to be honest and it could've turned intae one of they nights, but then I'm at the bar and I see this wee thing making eyes at me. Nice looking and all: I give it a couple of minutes, have another wee keek over her way to see she's still looking, then pitch up next to her wi a pint and a short, and one belter of a grin.

Turns out she'd taken her contacts out and her eyes wis sore and that's how come she wis staring at me like that. But I guess she liked the look of me anyways 'cause she let me buy her a drink. I wisnae saying no—the whole lot of them wis fit as you like, a bit skinny mind, but the arses on them. Aye, it's a tight arse for me any day.

So once I'd given her a wee bit of chat, making sure she wis at lest a wee bit intae it, I got Oli tae ditch his stool at the bar and we settled in beside them for some proper banter. English most of them, a girl from Italy and a guy from Norway or something, but the rest wis proper posh English, not too stuck up but. They wis only in the 'burgh another ten days or that, then a tour about and right back to London.

We wis a bit surprised like, but turned out the blokes wis all right and all. The muscles and hair on them and I'd pegged them as bummers for sure but turns out they wis right filthy bastards—got on wi Oli like they went to bloody primary school the gether or something. So I got to fire intae the wee Lucy wi the nice arse and big eyes. She keep up the chat fine and she wisnae loud or nowt, not at all like, but she wisnae shy neither if you ken what I mean.

I tried to hold back on the drink a bit, like you do when a cracker like that seems in reach, but she got me to buy her a Talisker—she'd never had it before—then another, and another. I snuck looks at her over ma tumbler. Her face wis all flushed like she'd been running or shagging or something. It suited her.

By the third whiskey she wis telling me about her cat. Her flatmate wis meant to be looking after the thing, and she wis right worried about it. I told her cats wis smart buggers: that one time ma mum's cat had pushed this cardboard box over and stood on it to open the cupboard where its food wis kept. Load of shite—but it made her feel better you ken. And, birds are mair likely tae come back tae the flats of cat lovers, after all. She wis smiling a lot in this way where her mouth wis kind of open, but even so, I knew I wis punching well above ma weight and wis bracing maself for a knock back.

She came though. Walked down the street like she'd known from the start that she wis going tae, sometimes close enough tae bang against the side of ma arm. We got a pizza from the wee place down the road from ma flat and she got stuck in like it wis the best thing she'd ever tasted. I wis feeling a bit rank at that point mind.

Turned out she like ma flat just fine though. I reckoned she felt the same about me so I made ma moves. Wisnae long till we were fucking like crazy. I've never had a girl move around so much. She wis right squirmy but at the same time she could do things like no one I'd ever been wi afore. I mean, I'd push her intae some kind of position, a leg up by her heid or whatever, and she'd just smile and hold it there. Afterwards I told her she wis the best lay I'd ever had and even meant it. She said I wisnae too shabby myself and fell asleep wi sweat still on her forehead. I lit a fag and lay there thinking about not so much, except that I wis right fucking knackered. And that it didnae feel half bad.

I kind of woke up in the morning—once when she wis running the shower and again when she wis messing up ma hair to say goodbye—but I didnae really realise she'd gone till the sun hit ma eyelids at about half ten and ma brain started to kick itself intae gear. What a dream eh? I went to work total cheesing, still thinking it wis nowt but a fantastic nae strings fuck at that point. But by half five I wis searching through the contacts on ma mobile phone and nae breathing till I found I'd saved her number. Asked for it before I knew it wis a sure thing she'd be coming back wi me. Not that it'd felt like much of a sure thing till she wis actually in ma bed like.

I called her on the walk home—after all they wisnae going to be in town much longer.

She didnae sound surprised to hear from me. There wis some tinkly piano music in the background and she wis out of breath, said she wis busy wi her rehearsal or some such and I thought I wis getting blown off, but then it suddenly wis that we were meeting in the Grassmarket at half ten, once she wis done wi her show.

I had a shave and put on ma best jeans afore going tae meet her, I dinnae mind saying I wis shiteing it a bit—I didnae ken what to expect sober.

Turned out that not only wis she fucking great in bed, but she could take a joke and all. And she could drink hard, she didnae mind getting sweaty and always smelled good anyways and she had these scratchy little calluses on her toes which should have been minging but wisnae. She laughed loud and she didnae care where she did it and everything I said wis funny. When I said something she especially liked she put her hand on ma arm too. Somehow it got to be that I met her at half ten the next few nights and all. And then, after another night that wis so damn guid I wanted to take pictures of it or something I got round to thinking that even though she wis going away, we might be onto a guid thing. Not that I brought it up, it wis just guid to think it.

On the Sunday morning I showed her around the town, pretending I wis a tour guide even though I didnae know the names of half the places, they're all just buildings you ken? And what did it matter 'cause she wis nodding and grinning away like it's all fascinating stuff. She asked me if I liked working down the garage and I shrugged—what's not to like? And she smiled this cute wee smile and to see her look like that made me feel right mushy. Aye, it wis a guid day. By the Monday I wis showing all the guys the picture I had of her on ma phone and couldn't wait to get out the lock-up and away.

On Wednesday she had a night off and I got her round tae have some dinner. Nowt fancy, but she said she wis right starved and that bangers and mash wis perfect. We wis sitting on ma bed wi a wee dram each when it came tae me proper that she only had two mair nights in the 'burgh. I wis thinking if I should say something but not really wanting tae when she told me she'd put a ticket aside for me if I wis up for coming tae her show on the morrow's night. Course I said I wis gagging to—'cause you kind of have to and, truth be told, I felt a bit bad I hadnae thought of it before. Not really ma kind of thing though, you ken, load of folks prancing around in their tights.

I spent the whole next day at work kind of fighting about it all in ma heid—whether I should cut ma losses at what's been a pretty fucking fantastic festival fling—or no. I thought about the way ma arm fit across the top of her shoulders when we wis walking and the way she pissed herself at ma shitty jokes. I thought about it and thought about it until Jim had to tell me to get a grip and get ma fucking mind back on the job. So I sucked it up and made a decision, I wis going to say I'd come down and visit when she wis back home. Like we could take it from there or whatever.

I hadn't even been in that theatre before but it still reminded me of being a kid, almost expected to put ma hand in ma pocket and pull out a packet of those winegums that ma mum always packed me off wi on school trips.

The seat felt too small and there wis a woman wi some sparkly shawl thing sitting next to me and sighing all over the place. I sat waiting for the lights to go out wi this weird feeling and all of a sudden I wanted someone to talk tae. But I just sat back and it got tae be so that I wis looking forward tae it by the time the curtains opened.

I'd seen some ballet and the like on the Christmas telly, like the one wi that woman dressed up like a fairy, so I thought I kent what I wis letting maself in for but this wisnae the same kind of thing at all. They wis all leaping about in skimpy outfits, but they looked angry, not all fernickity. The music wisnae like music either, not proper music, and the folks wis all grabbing each other and throwing themselves about like they wis trying to start a fight.

I didnae even recognise her at first, all stretched muscles and sharp eyes wi her hair scraped back. And then she dipped her heid to the side like I'd seen her do when we wis spraffing and I saw it wis her despite the lights that made her all green and purple. I half looked at the woman next to me, wanting to point Lucy out or something but the woman's face wis all dropped like some one that's just done a bucket or something and she never looked round at me.

Then the music went down all soft and the dancers started walking off the stage until wee Lucy wis the only one left up there. She stood there so sad, like she wis going to have a wailing fit any minute. Then she wis moving so slow and it wis so quiet I could hear the woman next to me breathing and I could hear mine was too fast and all. And still it wis so quiet, it got so I thought I wis going to burst out yelling or something. But I blinked and then, just like that, she wis firing around the place—spinning like crazy then holding this pose wi one leg right up in the air behind her—as though it wis nowt unusual. You couldnae see it in her face, you couldnae see the effort it wis costing her. I stared close, but there wis nowt there even though the sweat on her forehead and neck wis shining out.

The other dancers came back all in a rush, pushing and shoving until they made the big stage seem full and I couldnae quite see where she wis. Then I could. A couple of blokes swung her up and she perched on their shoulders, her arms in the air, and I could make out that she wis smiling this right big smile. A smile like she wis flying. A smile that made me think she knew how tae do that, how tae switch a smile on an off. Sat up there looking like the cat that got the cream. Aye, a big fucking smile alright, and it sucked all the smile right out of me.

I stood up and pushed ma way to the end of the row, people screwing their faces up as I go past and that uptight bitch huffing behind me. I didnae pay her any mind though, I wis just wanting out of there. I powered right on through, never even looked at the cute wee things on the door. Felt like I wanted tae keep going until that stupid fucking stage with its poncey twats and its bloody smiles was long gone, but I stopped in the street and lit up a fag. The bars would be open another few hours yet. Aye. I took a draw on ma fag and started walking, only turning ma heid to spit the taste out ma mouth.

FEATURED POET

KIMBERLY CAMPANELLO was born in Elkhart, Indiana, and she currently divides her time between London and Dublin. She earned an MFA in Creative Writing from the University of Alabama and is completing a PhD in Poetry at Middlesex University. Her work has appeared in journals in the USA, most recently in *The Cream City Review*. In 2009 she was a resident at the Fundación Valparaíso in Mojácar, Spain.

---

*

The squatters keep building tin houses
on my friend's land and he offers me
half its value if I go to Brazil with a machete
and some Portuguese and make them stop
for the next three years.
The squatters keep giving birth
without c-sections and use gravity
rather than forceps to let it all out.
The squatters keep breathing
in and out, in and out, *Sat Nam.*
Truth is our highest identity.
I am squatting over you, here, on the bed,
and godammit, I have to put *cunt*
in a poem one more time
because you are looking up at mine
saying, *Jesus.* To squat is to live free.
To squat is to trust that your insides
will get ripped out
in the best way possible.
To squat is to sink low at the knees,
but not lock them. To squat is to linger
and let the lips separate and speak
saying, *I can't imagine*
never having known you.

*

And the body lay born, beside the hacked off head.
—Ted Hughes

It's been a good day, I say, on 1st Ave., Little Haiti.
The goat was born easily and the moon
is wider than the widest high-rise
on the 41st street beach where Orthodox
Jewish women power walk in covered
hair and long black sleeves and skirts.
The youngest child shrieks at the goat
in more Kréyol than English,
and the eldest grabs my camera
insists on taking picture after
picture until he gets the right one.
In the end it's blurry and I look happy
next to the pigs sleeping in the boat
with its hull torn out. But we've made very little progress.
Or progress is a misnomer. Few of the neighbours
have doors and not because they have a different
definition of public and private.
I look to the placenta in the dust
and the bottle flies covering it.
Is there something to it? Clean and unclean.
The mother was supposed to eat it. The cord hangs
from the baby's gut, covered in its very first shit.
We all have to learn to shit neatly and not roll around in it
after. Does this thought obscure the freshness
of the moment? Little David wants to know the date,
October 4th, and he sings Happy Birthday.
The people missing limbs who line the streets here aren't fresh,
but they are tidily placed in people's memories
of the Papa Doc days. They aren't neat, but their stumps
end neatly. Someone shat on them
and walked away. Didn't roll around after.

*

D'aller là-bas vivre ensemble!/Aimer à loisir,/Aimer et mourir/Au pays qui te ressemble!
–Charles Baudelaire

I'm bleeding out on the Green
and there are ass bandits standing by waiting for someone better
with a hole less unpredictable, less full of teeth and silent screams.
I am bleeding out on the Green waiting
for a whole human being to emerge. But it's too soon.
Maybe I am that human. Maybe you are half of it.
Maybe there's nothing even
about what we might make.
Maybe I'm making human being
seem too important.

Workers are tossing gold geraniums into a barrel.
pulling them whole from the ground
and I keep seeing the same guy
wearing a dog collar everywhere I go. He has mud
on his velvet boots and he looks me in the eye
as if to say the mud is old mangoes and the mud is old
hearts and the mud is old books that I gave away or let rot.

There is space and there
is space
I tell you.

And there is disgrace.

In Germany they scrub out
their trashcans.

Old nature didn't ask for this.
To be the receptacle of our fantasies. Old nature didn't say
pick me to be the woman
turned into a map and charted and uncharted
for the sake of what you think you don't know.
Her *mons pubis* is the treasure land and her breasts the entryway.
A good thing cartographers knew something about foreplay.

I am bleeding out on the Green
and the Green could be anywhere
suffused with whatever meaning I say.

Like the Green is Florida's sea grape trees
with roots that trip me up as horseshoe crabs
flee my heavy *Fleurs du mal* step
and old women toss grapes into a bowl to make
sea grape jelly to scrape onto crackers for schoolchildren
to make them see the land is important, to keep them from building
more high rises, and boating over more manatees
and refusing to turn out their lights that make turtle
hatchlings march toward Wal-Mart
instead of the sea.

Or the Green is St. Stephen's in Dublin
where cops with long coats once shielded
men pissing straight liquor onto the grass
but never the women with blood on their thighs.
The best I could do is enter a pub
where the snug's walls have been taken down
now that women can be trusted to mingle
in the whole space and order their drinks at the bar
instead of through a little window with a sliding door.
But the snug is in my mind as they say.
A painful dialectic. The snug
is where you cut yourself down to half. Where you say no
to half, where you can say anything at all, and it's
of no consequence. There is space and there is
space I say. A useful dialectic. The snug is where you go
to talk about bleeding out on the Green. The snug is where you go
and keep yourself on guard. The snug is only in my mind. It's not real.
Right. I can do anything, go anywhere
and no one will touch me. Least of all when I am bleeding
out on the Green. Least of all when I am the old woman
picking sea grapes. Least of all when I am helping nature refuse.
When I am taking this blood right out.
When I am taking out a whole human. Being. Or a half. My half.

Or the Green is generality. As though that's possible.
The *Generalife* gardens of the Alhambra
where the flowing water is louder
than my mind where the snug is still built
louder than the ping of sea grapes
in the metal bowl. Step onto the Green.
Bleed out. Breathe out. In.

Kimberly Campanello

*

The Maya get arrested on South Beach
for sitting on a bench for too many days.
They're patted down, hands behind head,
as though their pockets contain nuclear waste
and their backpacks are iPhones of destruction
with applications that will drain our bank accounts,
steal our women, and leave dog shit unscooped.
Even the rich man watching it feels bad, tells me
they didn't have anywhere else to go.

That night I'm walking alone, drunk
on a mix of five countries' beers.
It's another night when just my presence
is a come hither, when my cunt
seems to be tattooed on my face.
I see the empty bench and I'm scared.
There are no Maya to watch over me
as though they had special
powers, as though I was important.

I do realise that I'm romanticising the Maya
and myself and that one day I will walk the streets
invisible, my old skin hanging from my
bones like money bags and the most
anyone will want from me is my wallet.
I just hope that same day the Maya
will be people, not just an image in a poem
whose arrest signals the end of civilization
or the rape of a rich white girl.

Kimberly Campanello

*

From the thousand responses of my heart, never to cease.
—Walt Whitman

I note the wreck of bodies all around me—ridges of cellulite
on thin thighs, breast implants gone astray, puffy wrists
and elbows, permanent brow furrows, the right soft hair
in all the wrong places, hair that's missing. In the sea
I cup a jellyfish in each palm and think of breasts,
how on women and men they are rocks to grab onto
as the sea tries to drag you out.

My friend told me once that he loved my skin,
that it expressed my freshness, my full heart.
But it's changing each day in this brutal sun
as I sit with my favorite books, freeing the poet, crossing off
lines of her poems so instead of begging him not to leave
she ends with, *I am alone. I must discover my heart/against rock.*

At the *Playa Piedra de Villazar* we square-danced in the water,
and I scraped my ankle on submerged rock. My skin,
my heart, against rock. Not being alone, I didn't really notice.
Did you notice the way I grabbed your chest
when we faced each other last? *Piel, corazón, piedra.*
I am alone. I must cross off something. Free
someone. Note the wreck of my body rocked.

Kimberly Campanello

*

We protect the weak and call it love
or ethics. For the safety of our students this door
must remain closed at all times. *Ani yalda tova. I am a good girl,* I tell the Israeli jeweler
who is impressed with my Hebrew. An American nearby says,
Fuck Israel. I offer, *I am a bad girl. Ani yalda ra.*

To dance is a kind of paralysis. Muscles contract
in a certain way and we call it beautiful.
The men on the beach made me think
they were dancing tango, but instead one
was helping the other will his feet to remember

walking. If I had withered hands and always gave you
your pen with my teeth would you think it beautiful?
For the continued safety of our money
these checkpoints must remain closed
at all times. For the quality of our progeny these legs

must remain closed at all times. These minds.
This mouth. This heart. Why don't you substitute
your for *these* and *this*? See how it feels. *Ani yalda ra.*
Feel that. Feel me feel you. Tell me I'm good
and bad. *Tova* and *Ra*. Let us be both.

Kimberly Campanello

*

He told me how in his childhood
vultures used to mean a rush out to the hay fields
to see what had died. The worst was when his father

mowed over the fawn. A fawn is taught, or maybe just knows,
to hold still in danger. This is usually for the best.
If I hold still, is it for the best? If I hold still, how will you come?

The fawn held still. The mower tore it to pieces.
The vultures came and with them, the children. The father wept.
The hay was baled to feed the cows for slaughter.

I rushed on my bike to the tower through spinning cities of gnats.
We met, and they died all over me, my face and arms speckled with black.
Not one was still. No one is still. Ever. Not me. Not you. Even the fawn breathed.

I am building this spinning city in a hay field.
You are rushing to its tower.
We will meet there, breathing, still.

Kimberly Campanello

IN THE SUMMER ISSUE

BANIPAL 38

ARAB AMERICAN AUTHORS

Etel Adnan, Naomi Shihab Nye, Khaled Mattawa, D H Melhem, Hayan Charara, Gregory Orfalea, Fady Joudah, Nathalie Handal, Randa Jarrar, Mohja Kahf, Patricia Sarrafian Ward, Sinan Antoon, Philip Metres, Assef al-Jundi, Deborah al-Najjar, Kadhim al-Hallaq, Lisa Suhair Majaj, Lawrence Joseph, Dunya Mikhail, Pauline Kaldas, Deema Shehabi, Lara Hamza, Susan Muaddi Darraj, Elmaz Abinader, Laila Halaby, Evelyn Shakir, Salah Awad, Iman Mersal, Jakleen Salam and Sargon Boulus

PLUS

A selection of modern Emirati poetry by

Khulood al-Mualla
Khalid al-Budoor
Nujoom al-Ghanem

www.banipal.co.uk

Micro-Cosmopolitanism

Michael Cronin

Seosamh Mac Grianna is on his way to Algeria when he changes his mind. The thought strikes him in London that instead of going to North Africa he should go instead to a country that is much nearer, but in a sense equally foreign, Wales. He explains his decision in terms of his own singular destiny as traveller and writer:

> Dar liom, goidé is fiú dom an ród mór leathan a shiúlas achan duine a leanstan? Ní hé mo bhealach é. Chan ar bhealach na gcarr agus na gcabhlach a gheobhas mise mo chinniúint. Bheadh leisc ar ainbhíosan a aidhmheáil go raibh sé riamh sa Bhreatain Bhig. In ainm Dé, siúil na háiteacha nach siúlann daoine eile, mura mbíodh le feiceáil agat ach tithe cearc. (Mac Grianna 1940: 83-84)
> [I think, what's the point of walking the big, wide road that everybody else follows? It is not my way. I will not find my destiny where cars and navvies go. An ignoramus would be reluctant to admit that he was ever in Wales. For God's sake, walk in places where nobody else walks, even if you see nothing but hen houses]

Mac Grianna took his own advice and travelled to Wales, an experience that would lead him to write a separate work on the country entitled simply *An Bhreatain Bheag*. However, not many Irish writers and intellectuals have followed the path trodden by Mac Grianna and as recently as 2000 M. Wynn Thomas in his prefatory remarks to a collection of essays on the literatures of Scotland, Wales and Ireland noted that, 'although there is ample evidence here of several of the cultures of the Anglo-Celtic archipelago speaking to each other, there is next to no evidence of them speaking empathically for each other—what is noticeable is that very few of the contributors have felt sufficiently confident in their knowledge of a neighbouring culture to venture to draw parallels, or at least to make comparisons, between that culture and their own'. What I want to suggest is a way of thinking about the cultures of countries like Wales and Ireland that is potentially of interest not just to those who wander off the beaten track of international travel but to those who throng the ród mór leathan, the big wide road, of contemporary writing.

Cosmopolitanism

It is commonly claimed that it was the Greek philosopher Diogenes who in the fourth century first defined himself as a citizen of the world. Later, Aristippus in a more evocative image expressed a similar idea by claiming that the road to Hades was the same distance from any point in the world. In 1552 Erasmus refused the citizenship of the city of the Zurich offered by Zwingli declaring that, 'I want to be a citizen not of one single city but of the whole world.' The ideal of humanity as a collection of free and equal beings, possessing the same basic rights and where notions of hospitality, openness to others and freedom of movement are primordial underlies much thinking about cultural contact and the intercultural from antiquity to our own times. Peter Coulmas, in his *Weltbürger: Geschichte einer Menscheitssehnsucht* (1990) offers the reader an historical overview of the vicissitudes of cosmopolitan thought down through the centuries and openly states his preference for a worldview which he believes to be the only one capable of ensuring lasting peace and friendship between the different peoples on the planet. For Coulmas, a decline in cosmopolitanism is always synonymous with the rise of particularism and the birth of nationalism. When he goes on to describe important moments in the history of cosmopolitanism, it is almost invariably in the context of great empires of yesteryear, the Greek, the Roman, the Byzantine, the Carolingian, the French, the Spanish, the Austro-Hungarian and the British. This approach is not particularly quixotic and it has become a historical commonplace to underline the multi-ethnic and multilingual character of empires, even if the focus is not as resolutely centred on the West as is the case with Coulmas. The version of cosmopolitanism made explicit by Coulmas is what we might term macro-cosmopolitanism, namely, a tendency to locate the cosmopolitan moment in the construction of empires, in the development of large nation-states (France, Great Britain, Germany) or more recently in the creation of supra-national organisations (European Union / United Nations / World Health Organisation).

For the macro-cosmopolitan, it is only large political units which are capable of allowing the development of a progressive and inclusive vision of humanity, even if occasional hegemonic over-reaching cannot be ruled out. Small nations, ethnic groups concerned with the protection or preservation of cultural identity, former colonies which still subscribe to an ideology of national liberation are dangerously suspect in this macroscopic conception of cosmopolitanism. Bloody conflicts in the Balkans and in Northern Ireland seemed to provide more recent justification for the distrust, in Pascalian terms, of the infinitely great for the infinitely small.

Coulmas evokes the popularity of the motto, 'small is beautiful', associating it with a fashionable interest in local costumes, dances and languages. His verdict is clear, 'this nostalgic looking back is clearly opposed to the onward march of history towards larger political entities'. Worse still, he declares, 'The small state is praised.' These small states have a function which is clearly described in a chapter on the great metropolises of history. The latter benefit from the arrival of immigrants from less important states, 'by means of this brain-drain, many brilliant minds escape their country of origin, particularly, small countries offering few possibilities.' In *Culture*, Raymond Williams offers a similar description of the role of the metropolis, with his notion that those who participated in the many avant-garde artistic groups were frequently, 'immigrants to such a metropolis, not only from outlying regions but from other and smaller national cultures, now seen as culturally provincial in relation to the metropolis.' Indeed, for Matthew Arnold in an earlier period it was precisely the centripetal pull of the centre that made the notion of separate nationhood for the Irish or the Welsh or the Bretons a dangerous illusion:

> Small nationalities inevitably gravitate towards the larger nationalities in their immediate neighbourhood. Their ultimate fusion is so natural and irresistible that even the sentiment of the absorbed race, ceases, with time, to struggle against it; the Cornishman and the Breton become, at last, in feeling as well as in political fact, an Englishman and a Frenchman (Arnold 1859: 71).

The existence of small countries is justified by their being a kind of pre-cosmopolitan nursery, a warehouse of the mind where cognitive raw materials await the necessary processing and polish of the present and former capitals of empires.

Micro-Cosmopolitanism

What I would like to propose here is a notion of micro-cosmopolitanism which will be opposed to that of macro-cosmopolitanism. Micro-cosmopolitan thought shares a number of macro-cosmopolitan core ideals (freedom / openness / tolerance / respect for the other) but it is distinctly different in foregrounding other perspectives, other areas of writing and reflection and above all in freeing cosmopolitanism from a historical vision and a set of ideological presuppositions that both threaten its survival as a necessary element of human self-understanding and its ability to speak meaningfully to many different political situations. Why do we need a micro-cosmopolitan perspective and what does it consist of? We will begin with the necessity for such a perspective.

There are now more nation states than at any other time in the world's history. Currently, none of these nations seem particularly keen on abandoning their independence and, in the case of countries like Tibet and Chechnya, the struggle for national independence still goes on. In this context, it is unlikely that small or new nations who have, often with great difficulty, freed themselves from a former colonial presence, will be particularly impressed by being told that the notion of nation is outdated and reactionary and that clinging to such a notion automatically disqualifies them from belonging to the cosmopolitan community. A dangerous and fatal consequence of this approach is to set up a progressive cosmopolitanism in opposition to a bigoted, essentialist nationalism where the latter has no place for the former. In other words, the inhabitants of smaller political units find themselves subject to the 'double bind' famously described by Gregory Bateson. Either you abandon any form of national identification, associated with the worst forms of irredentist prejudice and you embrace the cosmopolitan credo or you persist with a claim of national specificity and you place yourself outside the cosmopolitan pale, being by definition incapable of openness to the other. The effects of this particular double bind are particularly damaging and in cultural and political life bring about the paralysis that Bateson noted so clearly in our emotional lives. Extreme nationalists of all hues take refuge in virulent denunciations of anything construed to represent the cosmopolitan (as has been demonstrated in such a tragic fashion in European history by the history of Anti-Semitism) while the proponents of macro-cosmopolitanism for their part are trenchantly hostile to any movement of thought that might appear to harbour sympathy for nationalist ideology.

Another version of this unhelpful dualism is to be found in certain analyses of the phenomenon of globalisation. Globalisation is typically presented by its opponents as a process of whole-scale standardisation, dominated by large multinational corporations and international organisations such as the World Bank and the International Monetary Fund, acting at the behest of the political and economic interests of the world's remaining super-power, the United States. This thesis has been challenged by a number of thinkers such as Roland Robertson, Jonathan Friedman and Manuel Castells who view globalisation as much a fragmentary and centrifugal process as a unifying and centripetal one. Their analyses which would appear to challenge the hegemony of the powerful do not in fact offer smaller nations a particularly promising role as once again they are cast in the position of *fide defensor*, as the touchy and scrupulous guardians of national difference. The binarism of macro-cosmopolitan thinking—small, closed as against large, open—which also underlines Samuel Huntington's thesis on the clash of civilisations or Benjamin Barber's vision of 'Jihad vs. McWorld,' is deeply disabling intellectually and politically. Writers and intellectuals from nations such as Ireland, Scotland and Wales should not have to be condemned to the facile dualism of macro perspectives.

Micro-cosmopolitan thinking is an approach which does not involve the opposition of smaller political units to larger political units (national or transnational) but one which in the general context of the cosmopolitan ideals mentioned earlier seeks to diversify or complexify the smaller unit. In other words, it is a cosmopolitanism not from above but from below. The defence of difference is always problematic if the notion is understood in a essentialist and unitary sense but what I want to advance here is a defence of difference not beyond but within the national political unit. Micro-cosmopolitanism is linked to what I have called elsewhere fractal differentialism. This term expresses the notion of a cultural complexity which remains constant from the micro to the macro scale. That is to say, the same degree of diversity is to be found at the level of entities judged to be small or insignificant as at the level of large entities. Its origin lies in a paper published in 1977 by the French mathematician, Benoît Mandelbrot. Mandelbrot asked the following question, 'How Long is the Coast of Britain?' and his answer was that at one level the coast, was infinitely long. An observer from a satellite would make one guess that would be shorter than, say, a Paul Theroux negotiating every inlet, bay and cove on the coast and Theroux's guess would be shorter than that of a tiny insect having to negotiate every pebble. As James Gleick pointed out, 'Mandelbrot found that as the scale of measurement becomes smaller, the measured length of a coastline rises without limit, bays and peninsulas revealing ever smaller subbays and subpeninsualas at least down to atomic scales.' Mandelbrot's discovery was that the coastline had a characteristic degree of roughness or irregularity and that this degree remained constant across different scales. Mandelbrot called the new geometry that he had originated fractal geometry. The shapes or fractals in this new geometry allowed infinite length to be contained in finite space. The experience of the traveller bears out the discovery of the mathematician. The traveller on foot becomes aware of the immeasurable complexity of short distances in a way that is invisible to the traveller behind the windscreen or looking down from the air.

A particular striking example of the phenomenon is offered in the work of the English mathematician and cartographer Tim Robinson. In his *Stones of Aran: Labyrinth*, he offers a detailed exploration of the 14,000 fields that go to make up the island of Inishmore off the west coast of Ireland. What Robinson clearly demonstrates as he goes through field after field on this small island is not only the remarkable richness of these reduced spaces but also the omnipresence of the traces of foreignness, of other languages and cultures in a place that through the work of John Millington Synge and others was closely identified with Irish language and culture and Irish cultural nationalism. The local is honoured in Robinson's work but it is a local that is informed by diversity and difference. In a sense, it is the fractal travelling of the writer that allows for the elaboration of a theory of the micro-cosmopolitan.

Micro-cosmopolitanism helps thinkers from smaller nations to circumvent the terminal paralysis of identity logic not through a programmatic condemnation of elites ruling from above but through a patient undermining of conventional thinking from below. A micro-cosmopolitan perspective also avoids the ready assimilation of cosmopolitanism to economic and social privilege which is apparent not only in the tirades of the European Far Right but is present also in the analyses of progressive thinkers who are skeptical about the uses to which cosmopolitanism is put by transnational capital. Timothy Brennan, for example, launches a trenchant attack against cosmopolitan thinking in *At Home in the World: Cosmopolitanism Now* where he denounces the current vogue for cosmopolitanism as simply the well-meaning version of American imperialism which under cover of cultural pluralism wishes to ensure the continued dominance of its political, economic, military and cultural interests. Danilo Zolo in *Cosmopolis: Prospects for World Government* is similarly hostile:

> What western cosmopolitans call 'global civil society' in fact goes no further than a network of connections and functional interdepedencies which have developed within certain important sectors of the 'global market', above all finance, technology, automation, manufacturing industry and the service sector. Nor, moreover, does it go much beyond the optimistic expectation of affluent westerners to be able to feel universally recognised as citizens of the world—citizens of a welcoming, peaceful, ordered and democratic 'global village'—without for a moment or in any way ceasing to be 'themselves', i.e. western citizens.

The micro-cosmopolitan movement by situating diversity, difference, exchange at the micro-levels of society challenges the monopoly (real or imaginary) of a deracinated elite on cosmopolitan ideals by attempting to show that elsewhere is next door, in one's immediate environment.

City and Country

If there is a place that would seem to offer itself quite readily to the micro-cosmopolitan approach, it would appear to be the city. Lewis Mumford in 1961 was already claiming that the, 'global city is the world writ small, within its walls can be found every social class, every people, every language.' The cities that have been classed as the great world cities of the past have included Athens, Alexandria, Rome, Constantinople, Paris, Vienna, London, New York but now they include cities such as Karachi, Toyko, São Paolo, Mexico City and Montreal, to give some more recent examples. For certain thinkers such as Manuel Castells, Saskia Sassen and Gerard Delanty, the city, and in particular the large international metropolises are going to become more and more important at the expense of nation-states. These global metropolises, key nodes in international communication networks, by bringing together a plethora of different cultures, languages, identities, are seen as an inexhaustible reservoir for the renewal of the cosmopolitan spirit. Cities are indeed striking examples of the potential of a micro-cosmopolitan approach. The fact that between now and the end of the century more than 80% of the planet's population will be living in urban centres would seem to be yet another reason for favouring an exclusively urban focus in research.

The danger however is that we end up once again giving new life to a jaded binary opposition: town or country, progress or reaction. In this view, cosmopolitanism is the proper business of cities and the role of the rural population is to act as guarantors for the authenticity of the land. It has become a critical commonplace, for example, to show how the city of Dublin was marginalised in Irish writing for many years after independence because in the nationalist imagination the city was a foreign presence, an alien substance in the Irish body politic (Dublin—city of the Vikings, seat of British colonial power). The countryside alone was deemed worthy of interest by many of the post-independence short story writers because it was the countryside that was seen to be the incarnation of much that was deemed to be specific to Ireland. Needless to say, in Ireland, it was mainly urban intellectuals—Yeats, Synge, Standish O'Grady, George Moore—who contributed to the Romantic deification of the land in cultural nationalism. If the more extreme forms of nationalism see the city as the polluted well of the cosmopolitan destroying the manly vigour of the nation, the ready and too facile identification of the city with cosmopolitanism in the work of many thinkers on cosmopolitanism itself tends ironically to give succour to the most retrograde forms of nationalism.

One could argue that instead of arguing by implication and by default for a patriotism of the land, it is more enabling to argue for a cosmopolitanism of the land, in other words, to define specificity through and not against multiplicity. Casual observers of Irish set dancing in a pub in rural Clare, might properly feel that they are witnessing a practice which is deeply rooted in a locality but they are also seeing the fruit of the influence of French dancing masters who came to Ireland at the end of the eighteenth century, finding themselves unemployed due to the exile or untimely demise of their aristocratic patrons. More recently, Riverdance, for all its egregious excesses and Celticist parody, is a striking synthesis of Irish figure dancing and Hollywood musicals. To stress hybridity in non-urban settings is not to devalue but to revalue. A key element of the micro-cosmopolitan argument being advanced here is that diversity enriches a country, a people, a community but that diversity should not be opposed to identity from the point of view of a dismissive, macro-cosmopolitan moralism.

If we have insisted on the necessity of considering cosmopolitanism as a phenomenon that is not the unique preserve of the urban, the underlying concerns are partly eocological. It is unlikely that rampant urbanisation of both our societies and our planet is the best way for humanity to proceed. The accelerated drift from the countryside in these islands and throughout Europe is a factor that detracts from rather than enhances cultural diversity and represents a significant threat to linguistic diversity to name but one component of cultural specificity. It has become something of a critical commonplace in recent years for commentators on the writing of the smaller nations of the 'Anglo-Celtic archipelago' to resist the rurification of these literatures. In other words, there has been an understandable hostility to the depiction of Irish or Welsh or Scottish writing as providing accounts of picturesque, non-urban experiences for the jaded intellects of the metropolitan centres, non-metropolitan writing acting as a cultural alibi for the consuming passions of tourism. The insistence on the importance of the urban voice in contemporary Irish writing, of a tradition of describing town and city experience in Welsh-language poetry and prose and of the avatars of the urban sensibility in Scottish fiction are perfectly necessary correctives to the platitudes of the postcard. However, it is important that we do not lose sight of the considerable body of writing in English, Welsh, Irish Gaelic, Scots Gaelic and Scots which highlights the micro-cosmopolitan complexity of places and cultures which are outside the critical purview of the urban metropolis. In this way, in the investigation of the links between culture, place and language from the perspective of the fractal differentialism mentioned earlier it will be possible to develop a reading of, for example, Irish, Welsh, Scottish rural experience which is not condemned to a wistful *passéisme* but is forward-looking in its restoration of political complexity and cultural dynamism to areas of Irish, Welsh, Scottish territory and memory. Such a move, an integral part of the micro-cosmopolitan project, would both revitalise enquiry into a substantial body of our respective literatures but would also have important implications for the development of a progressive literary and cultural criticism in dealing with rural communities throughout the world.

Particularism is easily parodied. A concern with specific places or peoples or cultures can appear more limiting or indeed narcissistic than a more universal, abstract compassion for all of nature, or all of humanity. The philosopher Val Plumwood argues, however, that care for or empathy with specific aspects of nature rather than with nature as an abstraction is vital if there is to be any substance or commitment to our concern. As she observes, '[c]are and responsibility for particular animals, trees and rivers that are well known, loved, and appropriately connected to the self are an important basis for acquiring a wider, more generalised concern.' The major drawback with finding particular attachments to be ethically suspect and advocating instead a genuine, 'impartial' identification with nature or with the good, however defined, is that one can end up favouring an indiscriminate identification which subverts the basis for the initial concern i.e. the desire to preserve difference. Plumwood comments:

> this "transpersonal" identification is so indiscriminate and intent on denying particular meanings, it cannot allow for the deep and highly particularistic attachment to place that has motivated both the passion of many modern conservationists and the love of many indigenous peoples for their land.

If we transfer our attention from biodiversity to cultural ecology it is possible to measure the particular importance of writings that are focused on a specific place, such as Ireland, but which are equally alert to the news from elsewhere. What Plumwood intimates is that it is the micro-cosmopolitanism of the margin rather than the macro-cosmopolitanism of the centre that allows for a cultural politics which is crucially re-centred but not ultimately self-centred. The danger with the ród mór leathan is that it may ultimately lead nowehere.

Works Cited

Arnold, Matthew. 'England and the Italian Question.' *The Complete Prose Works*. Ed. R.H. Super. Ann Arbor: U. of Michigan Press, 1961. vol. 1, 71.

Bateson, Gregory. "Double Bind." *Steps to an Ecology of Mind.* London: Paladin, 1973. 242-249.

Barber, Benjamin. *Jihad vs. McWorld*. New York: Ballantine Press, 1996.

Castells, Manuel. *The Rise of the Network Society*. Oxford: Blackwell, 1997.

Coulmas, Peter. *Weltbürger: Geschicte einer Menschheitssehnsucht*. Reinbek: Rowohlt, 1990.

Cronin, Michael. *Across the Lines: Travel, Language, Translation*. Cork: Cork University Press, 2000.

Delanty, Gerard. *Citizenship in a Global Age*. Buckingham: Open University Press, 2000. 99-102.

Fernández Armesto, Felipe. *Millennium: A History of Our Last Thousand Years*. London: Black Swan, 1996.

Gleick, James. *Chaos: Making a New Science*. London: Cardinal, 1987.

Huizinga, Johann. 'Erasmus über Vaterland und Nationen.' *Gedenkschrift zum 400. Todestag des Erasmus von Rotterdam*. Trans. mine. Basel: Verlag Braus-Riggenbach, 1936. 34.

Huntington, Samuel, 'The Clash of Civilizations.' *Foreign Affairs*. 72(3). 1993. 22-50.

Mac Grianna, Seosamh. *Mo Bhealach Féin*. Baile Átha Cliath: Oifig an tSoláthair, 1940.

-----. *An Bhreatain Bheag*. Baile Átha Cliath: Oifig an tSoláthair, 1937.

Mumford, Lewis. *The City in History*. London: Penguin, 1991.

Plumwood, Val. 'Nature, Self, and Gender: Feminism, Environmental Philosophy and the Critique of Rationalism.' Eds. L. Gruen and D. Jamieson. *Reflections on Nature: Readings in Environmental Philosophy*. Oxford: Oxford University Press, 1994.

Ritzer, George. *The McDonaldization of Society*. Thousand Oaks (Cal.): Pine Forge Press, 1993.

Robinson, Tim. *Stones of Aran: Labyrinth*. Dublin: Lilliput Press, 1995.

Saskia Sassen. 'The State and the Global City.' *Globalization and Its Discontents*. New York: The New Press, 1998.

Williams, Raymond. *Culture*. London: Fontana, 1981.

Wynn Thomas, M. 'Introduction.' Eds. Tony Brown and Russell Stephens. *Nations and Relations: Writing Across the British Isles*. Cardiff: New Welsh Review, 2000.

Zolo, Danilo. *Cosmopolis: Prospects for World Government*. Trans. David McKie. Cambridge: Polity Press, 1997.

Bud

In the scattered wood she wraps her arms against
the wind in hope of keeping safe
what is already gone.

She stops at intervals to check new growth.
Ash holds tips like the tiny black hoofs
of a miniature goat.

Beech is budded in overlapping folds of
copper, elegant as a slender woman
sheathed in silk.

Chestnut branches bulge, vulgar,
fat with promise, expectant.
She blinks, looks away.

Crab apple's bark is ancient, wrinkled.
Buds look dead. She swallows and
moves on.

Holly wears clusters of grapes for a doll's house,
foetal berries along each stem.
Her belly jags.

Nicola Griffin

Shadows in a Glass

Leona Cully

A week after Tom Walsh was shot in the back, the man who murdered him knocks on our door.

'I hear your father's in hospital,' he says. He won't look me in the eye, stares at my bare feet in flip flops, at the chipped blue varnish on my toenails. Car doors slam in front of the chippers across the road. A woman and three children go inside. The smell of burnt grease, cut with vinegar, overhangs the street. There's no wind out but there's a nip in the air. Summer is over. A man walking a dog passes and glances at us. One of the Dublin crowd, from the new estate at the end of the town. I only know him to see.

Dermot Clancy, I do know. I heard he'd got out on bail but it's a shock to see him walking around. I haven't seen him since Midnight Mass on Christmas Eve, what eight, nine months ago? He was with a new woman, Bernie Lynch, who had bleached her hair since I saw her last. Later, in the pub he sat in the corner with her, unsmiling, but then he never smiled much. I've been keeping away from the pub this year, and from what I heard so had he. Until last week.

I can't think what it is he wants.

'Your doorbell is broken. I had to knock.'

'It's been that way for years,' I say.

'Oh, right. So how is your father?' he says as if he's reading from a script.

'Not great,' I say. My feet are cold. I shiver, like someone just walked over my grave, as my mother used to say.

'Sorry to hear that,' he says. 'They can do a lot these days. A heart attack isn't the end of the world anymore.' He smiles at me but it doesn't reach his eyes.

'It's not his heart. He had a brain aneurysm.'

'Oh,' he says, 'I didn't know.' He looks down the street as if he's waiting for someone to prompt him his lines. Town is quiet. The evening is drawing in, darkening slowly. He looks so harmless standing there in his Sunday best. Charcoal grey trousers, polished black shoes, a navy jacket zipped right up as if the zips and laces and seams of his clothes are holding him together. I think of Tom running across that field, scared out of his wits, waiting for the explosion, and then falling down, down into the dark grass.

Clancy's always had a temper, even in school, and it only got worse as he got older. He tried to kiss me once, at a disco. He was very drunk, and I'm not sure he knew who he was grabbing. You got used to pushing drunk men off you at the end of a night. Their eyes full of lust and hate. Clancy wasn't the worst of them. Fellas provoked him because it was so easy to wind him up. I was there the night he glassed Johnny Kelly in the Roxy. Kelly, with blood pouring down into his eyes, had to be held back from going after Clancy again. A couple of stitches, a couple of months later, and they made up again. Men are strange that way.

And here's Dermot Clancy at my door, trying to make small talk.

'Is Luke in?' he asks.

'Not at the minute. He'll be home soon though.'

That's a lie. I'm wary of him, don't want him to know I'm alone for hours yet. Luke won't be home till well after midnight. Late night shopping, lots of shelves to stack. He's an electrician by trade but that work's all dried up. Truth is, Luke probably won't be home at all because he'll head over to his girlfriend's house. Clancy must be desperate for a friend. My brother was in his class at primary school but they were never close.

All I want is to go back inside, watch my programmes, have another smoke in peace.

'Why don't you—'

'I was thinking I could drive you. You know. To visit your Dad when Luke's working. Or to the shops. Or to work. If you need a lift,' he says, each word an effort. He chances a quick look at me. His eyes are glassy, like he's on something.

'We'll manage,' I say.

'It's no trouble. I hear your car's off the road.'

I know what he wants now. His mother's sent him to do his penance, to look good before the trial. Mrs Clancy had been good to Mammy before she died, as well she should. Didn't Mammy clean her house for years. I think of Mrs Clancy, how her carefully made-up face must have crumpled when she heard what her son had done.

Two girls walk by very slowly, and stare at Clancy, then me. Dagger looks for both of us. He'll have at least a year of signing on at the Garda station, of being glared at, and maybe worse. I don't want any trouble, and it doesn't look like he's going to take no for an answer.

'Come in for a minute,' I say, and soon as I've said it I'm sorry.

He follows me in, sits down at the kitchen table.

'A cup of tea?'

He nods. He's pale as a ghost.

I fill the kettle and look out the window. It's dark now. I can see our reflections in the glass. We look crooked, the panes of glass are so old and warped.

The story I heard is that Clancy and Tom spent all day drinking together last Bank Holiday Monday. Clancy insisted he'd drive them to Roxy's because the taxis were all busy. They planned to stop at Tom's house so he could get some cash but they had a huge row. Clancy kicked him out of the car just before they got to his house. What happened next seemingly is Clancy drove home to grab the sawn-off shotgun he kept hidden under his bed. The girlfriend was frantic trying to stop him but he wouldn't listen. He drove all the way back to Tom's and banged on the door, shouting for Tom to come out, he was going to blast his head off.

Tom took off, out the back door, and across the fields.

Clancy ran after him, stopped and fired.

They say the guards found Clancy sitting on the grass, near Tom's body, in the moonlight, sobbing, saying over and over that he hadn't meant to shoot him just scare him.

That's the story I heard anyways but you never know what to believe.

I leave the TV on but turn the volume down low. I offer him a Benson and Hedges.

'I don't smoke,' he says.

I stay standing, leaning against the kitchen counter. I light a cigarette and realise that my hands are shaking. None of the stories I've heard mention Tom's mother. I imagine her kneeling by her son's body, shielding him, too late, wishing she could close up the hole in Tom's chest with her hands. Listening to the sound of his last, choked breath.

Clancy's sitting at the kitchen table, his right leg jigging a mile a minute. His eyes flit around the kitchen as if he's looking for an escape route.

The kettle boils.

I turn my back on him and make a lot of noise with cups and saucers. Saucers. We never use saucers. I bring him over a cup of tea that looks grey it's so weak. I put the milk carton and the sugar bowl down beside him.

'Thanks,' he says but he doesn't touch it. He's hunched over, staring down at the worn lino under his feet, scuffs over an old cigarette burn.

'You still seeing Matty Moore?' he asks.

'No,' I say. 'That's long over.'

'He wasn't your type anyway,' he says, and he laughs.

My phone's on the counter. I pick it up. No messages but I pretend to read one.

Everyone knew Matty preferred the pub to my company. When he's had enough of the bar stool, before all his hair falls out, Matty'll make a dash for the youngest girl who'll have him. You'd be surprised how often that works, auld fellas with girls fifteen, twenty years younger than them. The girls are all desperate to settle down still, in this age of having it all and sex toys and empowerment, whatever the hell that is.

I stub out my cigarette, put my phone in the pocket of my sweats. Before I've even thought about it, I say, 'How's Bernie?'

He looks stricken. I feel bad because I asked that on purpose. For all I know she'll come back to him when he gets out, she's so desperate to get a ring on her finger.

An ad promising to pay great prices for gold jewellery comes on the telly.

'Everyone's mad for gold these days. All those break-ins recently, they're ransacking houses for gold jewellery,' he says. He's trying to smile again, has straightened up, trying to make an effort to chat.

I turn off the TV. A long uncomfortable silence might get him out of here.

'How's work?' he tries.

'I'm signing on ,' I say, and he reddens at that. At that.

'Oh,' he says. 'Sorry. I've been busy with the house. And work. It's hard to keep up with all the news.' He stares at me. He doesn't look well. This close up, I notice how much he's failed, the white in his hair, a grey tinge to his face. Fading away, like the people in my father's black and white photos from the fifties. All those dog-eared photos of blurry ghosts.

His eyes dip and flick over my breasts. I'm just wearing an old vest top and sweats. I cross my arms.

'Not much work around,' he says much too loudly.

'No,' I say back, annoyed.

It was alright for him. Went to college and all that, had a good job up to last week. Worked in that big American place thirty miles away. I can never remember exactly what it is he does. Something technical. I think he has to wear one of those white suits with feet and a hood, like a giant babygro. A factory of giant babies. Clancy's the kind of guy people say comes from a good family by which they mean a well-off family. Me and Luke are not from that kind of family. People used say Mammy was a saint for all she put up with but she couldn't keep us in school past fifteen so that let her down. Then she took to hounding me not to get pregnant. You're skirt's too short, your top's too low, you look like a tart, every time I stepped out the door.

Leave her alone, said Daddy, she looks very glamorous, like one of them models in the paper. In the pub, he'd boast about his good-looking daughter and ask if anyone could offer him a hefty dowry. One night, I was in the same pub as him and I heard him at it again so I went up to him and told him to quit it. He slapped me on the arse, his own daughter, and almost fell off the stool he was that stocious. After that I changed the way I dressed, I was sick of the grief and the attention. I copied the style of the girls who came home from Dublin at the weekends. The vet's son asked me out the following summer. Mammy thought all her Christmases had come at once.

'Are you cold?' Clancy asks because I'm rubbing my arms. 'What kind of music do you listen to?'

And I'm thinking that he's just not right in the head, the way he's jumping from subject to subject. I decide the best thing to do is play along, keep it light, and figure out a way to ask him to leave without aggravating him.

'Neil Young. Crosby Stills and Nash. Kings of Leon. Credence Clearwater Revival. That kind of thing.'

I take my phone out of my pocket and text Luke that Clancy called for a visit and I'm a bit nervous.

'Neil Young? He's a bit old hat, isn't he?' he says like he's flirting with me.

The vet's son hated my taste in music. He was the first guy who actually asked me out on a date. Guys asked you to dance when they were drunk, you kissed on the dance floor, let them feel you up a bit. Then the battle began to get you outside into the car, or their friend's car, or the alley. I kissed a lot of guys but seldom went back to their cars. As soon as a girl had sex with a guy who wasn't a boyfriend everyone called her a bike, a slut, behind her back. I only fooled around in cars until I went with the vet's son. His kisses were slow, deep, our teeth grinding on each other, teeth on my throat, persuasive hands under me. In his father's car, he'd let down the front passenger seat, and I'd climb on top of him, my hair falling over his face. I thought, before him, that only I could make myself come. When I broke it off with him, Mammy was devastated. You could see she had built up a rosy future with me ensconced in a big house, a granny flat stuck on for her, grandkids running around. Probably imagined one of those big houses with the wraparound drives and the stonework fronts. Clancy built a house like that, three stories high. Our ancient bungalow would fit into his kitchen.

My phone beeps.

Wots he want?? Get him out. Call me & i talk 2 him

'Who are you texting?' asks Clancy in a pleasant voice, like we're best friends.

'Luke,' I say.

'Luke's sound,' says Clancy. 'I hear he's a good electrician. Shame he's struggling. Will he head off to Australia? You have any plans yourself?'

I rub a smear of old make-up off my phone. The display screen feels rough under my thumb, scarred and scratched.

'No plans,' I say.

I went to London once but only lasted a fortnight. My girlfriends tried to talk me into staying but I couldn't stick it. I like to see faces I know, who know me. People who can help you out when you're stuck, and you help them, if you can. I thought I was smart training as a beautician after years of working in grocery shops, clothes shops, furniture shops. Got a job in the beautician's which opened up a few doors down from our house. Brenda's Beauty Shop lasted a year. We cried when we closed the doors on the last day.

I top up my dole doing bikini waxes and fake tans in the living room, but I have to make sure Daddy's out of the way before the women come in. Although that's not a problem now he's sick. Really sick.

I have goose bumps on my arms.

'I'll just get a jumper,' I say.

I have to walk past him to get to the door that leads to the back of the house. In the hall, I look back at him through the half-open door and see him pick a jar up off the table. He reads the label, and hastily puts it back. He blushes right down to his neck. Blushes.

I pull on an old hoodie top, and think at least there's some satisfaction in a man's embarrassment at the hidden lives of women. The work some women do on themselves would make you wall-fallen tired just thinking about it. They want to be plucked, waxed smooth, sprayed and stained until their skin looks like hard plastic. I see them looking at me and thinking she's a bit scruffy for this lark. Yesterday I didn't cool the wax enough and scorched a woman's thigh. I don't think she'll be back.

The vet's son used laugh at me and say, You want to waste your life in this hole? I figured I was just a summer fling for him so I broke it off before he went back to college, to finish learning how to stick his hand up a cow's arse. Like father, like son. Back to mix with his own crowd, to find a nice wife. At Mass once his mother gave me a look that left me in no doubt what she thought of me. He wasn't like that, the vet's son, but he annoyed me with snide remarks about my taste in music, films, TV programmes, or the fact that I had no ambition. What's wrong with sticking with a place through thick and thin, I said, with a town you know inside out but the people in it always surprise you sooner or later?

Though you could do without the kind of surprise Clancy gave Tom and his mother. At the funeral, just a few days ago, Mrs Walsh walked up to the coffin, touched it briefly, then sat down. Just a neighbour beside her to comfort her. On her way out of the church, after we'd paid our respects, she stopped where Mr and Mrs Clancy sat at the very back. They hadn't gone up to her. She shook Mrs Clancy's hand, then Mr Clancy's, nodded and followed the coffin out of the gloom of the church. Mrs Clancy stayed a long time, kneeling in that pew, head bowed. I was amongst the last to leave and saw Mr Clancy help her up. Her face was streaked with mascara, pink lipstick bleeding from the edges of her mouth.

I nip into the bathroom to use the loo. When I'm washing my hands, I look in the mirror, then look away again. I'm not wearing make-up today and without it I look tired, rubbed out.

I have to get him out of the house. My plan is to barge back in, all bluster, and tell him thanks for calling and we'll let you know tomorrow if we need a lift, thanks.

Through the open door I see him cradling his head in his hands, fingers scrubbing at his temples.

He killed his friend, goes through my mind. His friend.

Tom was the quiet, witty type. We had a fling when I was seventeen, and he was twenty-four. He made me laugh but he liked to start a fight when he had a lot of drink on him. One night he was squaring up to some fella and I tried to pull him away and the look he gave me froze my blood. I walked away and left him to it and he wouldn't speak to me after that, as if I'd unmanned him or something.

I go back into the kitchen.

'You alright?' I ask.

He doesn't answer, or look up.

Why did I invite him in? To see what's it like to talk to a murderer? It's disappointing I'll tell you that. He's just a man with terror in his eyes who can't rewind the past.

'Look,' I say, 'why don't you head home? We'll think about the lifts. Give you a call tomorrow.'

Before he can answer, something smashes through the kitchen window.

Clancy jumps in his seat, then freezes.

'Jesus,' I shout.

My heart is pounding but I run to open the front door and step outside onto the footpath and look around. A flash of jeans and white trainers jumping over a wall, down past the chippers. I can guess who it is. Tom's cousin. He only lives a few doors down, in the other direction. He's seen Clancy knocking on our door, or someone's told him. Now my name will be dirt around town.

I go back inside and close the door. Clancy is still sitting at the table, frozen to the spot.

'Who was it?' he asks.

'I don't know,' I say, anger rising in me.

'It's my fault. I'm sorry.'

I inspect the damage. A large stone smashed through one pane of glass.

'I'll help you clean it up,' he says.

'No. I'll do it,' I snap back.

I sweep glass off the window sill and draining board with a brush and pan. Shards still hang in the frame, and I smash them out with the handle of the brush.

He says, 'I'm sorry. I'm so sorry. I'll fix the window tomorrow. It's one of the old sash windows isn't it? Just the one pane. Get me some cardboard and gaffer tape and I'll board it up for now. Tomorrow I'll get some glass cut and buy some putty. Do they still sell putty?' and he looks at me and he's sobbing.

I go out the back door to put the glass into the recycling box where we put beer and wine bottles. Which makes no sense. Now I've put shards of glass amongst the bottles and I'll probably cut my finger when I'm putting the bottles into the bottle bank which is a chore I love, all those satisfying crashes and explosions.

A while back, after a visit to the bottle bank, I went into the shopping centre to wait for Luke and I ran into the vet's son, who has his own practice in that town. I hadn't seen him for years and I'd imagined he'd be fat and balding but he looked good. Those wide, angular shoulders I had left teeth marks on. He smiled at me but didn't stop to say hello. A woman with expensive blonde hair called him to help her with a buggy and shopping bags. Before he went to give her a hand, he gave me a look that made me walk on as fast as I could, past the boarded up shops, the Cash for Gold booth, and out into the rain.

I pick up a wine bottle and swing it hard against the back wall of our house. Open my eyes and I'm holding the jagged neck, and there's green glass all over my feet. I shake the splinters off my feet, throw the bottle neck into the box. My heart is pounding.

I go back inside. He's still sitting there but he's stopped crying.

'Can I have a smoke? I need a smoke,' he says. He's trembling.

I put a cigarette into my mouth and light it for him, walk over to him and put it into his hand. His nails are bitten down to the quick. He puts it to his lips and draws on it but doesn't inhale, just blows out a cloud of smoke.

I light my own cigarette, and sit down in the armchair beside the unlit range.

'Do you remember the time,' he says, 'when they tried to set up a rounders tournament in town?'

I nod though I barely remember that, I was only fifteen or thereabouts.

'I was having a huge row with the team captains about the rules?' He's looking at me like he expects me to fill in the gaps.

I shrug.

'Everyone was sitting around on the pitch and then you stood up and said why are we wasting time listening to him, can we not just get on with the game and they all clapped and I walked away.'

'Did I? I don't remember that. You sure that was me?' I say but I do remember now, and I don't like the way he's looking at me.

I look away from him, start deleting old messages from my phone.

'You must remember,' he says loudly, and he's leaning forward.

'Well, I don't,' I say. I wonder if I should call Luke.

'I think you do,' he says.

He stabs his cigarette out on the saucer, once, twice, three times and the saucer rattles and he knocks over the cup of tea.

'Shit,' he says, and stands up.

Pale tea spills out over the dark scarred wood of the table like a deformed hand, fingers creeping towards him. He steers the liquid away from him with the side of his hand but then it falls in several thin streams onto the lino with an obscene dribble. Cupping his palms, he tries to catch the tea, but it's no use, and he gives up. Shakes his hands and wipes them on his trousers.

He's looking at me like it's all my fault.

I stand up, pull my hoodie on tighter, zip it up. I go over to the counter, throw him a dishcloth which stinks.

'Clean that up,' I say. 'I'll be back in a minute.'

I grab a torch and go out the back, to the shed, to search for some cardboard and tape to patch up the window.

Her way of saying no

Andrew Meehan

On duty Chloe Vars is unrecognisable. She cannot function if she allows herself to think of her boyfriend Joao and if she does allow herself to think of him when she is on duty she makes it clear to herself that he has not left to live in Portugal but is in the room next door polishing wine glasses so that they shine like lasers, and if they talk it is to discuss lemons or ice.

When she signed up for the job that took her from Nimes to Faro to Macau, Macau to Hamburg and then to a celebrated hotel in Connemara, Chloe wanted things to be perfect. Though she begins with an uninterrupted walk through the hotel grounds she knows today will not be perfect and will end in shame. There is a small wedding party arriving and she is not looking forward to the expectations and illogical questions that will turn her hotel into something like the end of the world. She ends her unstressed walk carefully crying under a dripping tree.

She hopes for word from Joao, who left quickly for another barman's job at a resort near Lisbon, obliging Chloe to deal with his belongings before moving into her single room in the staff accommodation. She gets to the office and sees there is nothing from Portugal; only a call from the wedding photographer.

'You know when I said I was having problems getting the horse for today's photograph?'

'Please don't say you're not going to do what you said you would do,' says Chloe.

'You're confusing me now. I'm not saying that I'm not going to do anything.'

'What did you say to me when I asked you for this horse?'

'I can't remember?'

'You said yes. So where is it?'

'I don't know.'

Short of time, unaccountably tired, and weighed with anxiety about Joao, even down to his whereabouts and well-being, Chloe hustles the delivery of a horse from a local riding school. From the office window she looks out at a lone fisherman in a tiny boat on the river. She once saw him fall out of his boat reaching for a leaping salmon and she thinks of it now.

She works so hard and sets such high standards that an unsuspecting country hotel, prized for its dreamlike setting, can hardly be blamed for her unease, a truth she mistrusts but cannot deny. She has suffocated the vagueness about when Joao might return with a certainty that she has a job to do, allowing herself security of one kind if not another. She finds herself surrounded by his fishing rods and nets and waders, birthday and Christmas presents that were at first adored then casually abandoned. Now, she fears that his belongings are hers. She wonders if he is missing his things.

Lately, in boredom, she has found herself whistling and sweeping, smoothing out cling-film in the hope of reusing it. She can't bear the silence at night, the bed pressing against her. There are mice, a team of capering bats, whose squeaks have become an invitation to something sexual: she often imagines they are in the room with her, but refuses to be afraid of bats. She refuses to fear the stillness, the mindless night. She imagines the silent river, the tunnel of sleep, a squeak and then morning.

There is an American, a man called Bill Disk, in the lobby. He drives her crazy by talking to her in a French so earnest and correct that she pities him.

Bill Disk takes care to repeat that it is his second but his wife-to-be's first marriage; once to remind her who is in charge of whom, twice to make it clear that it is not a normal wedding with invited guests, and three times to spell out that it may be a no-fuss wedding but it will be a perfect wedding. Chloe doubts it will be perfect.

'Can I offer you something to drink?' she says.

'At this hour?' he says. He is blandly handsome and as pale as pastry, or margarine.

'Perhaps we'll send some coffee and home-made pastries to your room?'

'Not one bit hungry.'

'Just the coffee?'

'Keeps me up.'

Chloe, who normally prides herself on delivering the pure moment of welcome, says something airy.

'Does this place work?' he asks. 'The water's brown.'

'This is normal,' she says.

The language barrier is an advantage in some situations. However, her desire to be clearly understood and Joao's inability to clearly understand seems to be the reason her room is still full of his unwanted belongings. He was Portuguese, she was French, they communicated in English, and the more she tried the less he understood, until now, when he appears not to even hear. On the phone, she can hear him being quiet, this is what it has come to. It has become a kind of numbness, a hypothermia.

Then something strange. Bill Disk's beautiful but ratty bride-to-be Marion Bishop arrives. She flutters her fingers, looks over her shoulder impishly and, like it's a Frisbee, flies her hat across the lobby where it comes to rest on a lamp. Then she pops her collar and rolls her shoulders as if expecting applause.

Chloe crosses the lobby and wordlessly places the hat on a rack by the front door and instructs O____, the porter, to be especially careful with the luggage. She expects to see Marion Bishop bursting into flames at the top of the stairs before cart-wheeling into her room. Chloe's life seems innocuous by comparison. She takes some soup to her room but her curiosity about Bill Disk and Marion Bishop won't subside. In bed, she fixates on Bill, his fiancée, and carefully imagining their lives and landscapes, the reasons for marrying in a cold castle far from home, far from anywhere, the all-powerful dreams that compel you to transport you and your wedding cake five thousand miles, and, slowly giving in to the irresponsible dream that Joao will return with infinite apologies, Chloe, grinning, giggling, mimicking Marion Bishop's shoulder-roll, lies awake until dawn.

She delivers Marion Bishop's breakfast to her suite.

'With our compliments,' says Chloe.

'Tell me you brought the coffee?'

'With pleasure.'

'Keep it coming. This is the finest castle in Ireland, right?' she says.

Marion Bishop is disappointed the castle is so cementy: it reminds her of a huge elephant or the surface of a distant planet or just too much cement. On the silent TV, on a cookery show set somewhere in southern Europe, a family is having a faithfully recreated Sunday lunch. The scene contains women with unpinned hair, in hats like Marion Bishop's, battered pots and much-used bowls full of fennel and lentils. An old man is dancing with his granddaughter, and somewhere in the scene, Marion Bishop, or is it Chloe, hesitates then kicks away her sandals.

Marion Bishop runs a bath. She asks Chloe to stay. She wants company, another faithfully recreated scene of comfort and confidentiality. The way Marion Bishop fixes the bathroom door so that they can continue to talk easily and then steps into the bath so that she can prepare to be married and her cloudless life will start. It was the way Marion Bishop caught Bill Disk's eye before she threw the hat across the lobby, it is the way she smiles when Chloe mentions his name now. Chloe sees Marion Bishop's eyes close with this soft talk of marriage and in the bedroom she sees the hat, Marion Bishop's neat white trouser suit she would like to wear herself but won't, and knows already that she will take pleasure in breaking this stranger's marriage apart. She excuses herself to check on news of the horse.

'Did you misunderstand the word horse?' says Bill Disk.

Chloe disintegrates when she sees it: the horse is so puny she could wrestle it to the ground herself. 'There was no misunderstanding,' she says.

'It is not as if I asked for a ship in a bottle.'

It is not in her nature to refuse to oblige a guest. It is in her nature to say yes. She arranges for extra flowers, more champagne, cigars, a harpist, but cannot manage to find a horse that doesn't look like it has just had a stroke. Worn-out and cautious and chaotic with failure she feels something harden: the hypothermia again, and briefly she considers just leaving; a bus and a plane tonight and a train in the morning and she can be in Nimes by lunchtime. She knows the schedules. She stands in the office and frets until V____, the hotel owner, calls to say she is employee of the month; but this and bouquets and thank-you notes and compliments of any kind seem to her now to be like sunlight she is aware of but cannot feel.

Bill Disk returns from his wedding à deux and delivers a speech to anyone who will listen: 'Me and my new wife will live to a hundred. We'll eat our greens. We'll eat our greens and on weekends you won't see us for dust because we'll be drunk and in bed.'

Bill Disk and Marion Bishop dance before dinner; proper frothy dancing and when it subsides Chloe assigns one waiter to Bill Disk, another to his new wife and terrorises them both into slickness, freezes them into it. She cleans glasses and wonders if Joao is sleeping with M____ again and good for him if he is, if that's what it takes. If he can find someone to put up with his constant stupidity, good for him. Chloe feels brutish and unwomanly since Joao has gone.

She is in her office enjoying a heap of well-travelled wedding cake when, inexplicably, Bill Disk appears and begins to talk. About who hasn't made the journey from Seattle, can he blame them? About all the beautiful food, which isn't what he expected at all, after the brown water. About, he supposes, being married. About addressing certain issues, tiresome issues, that he has no interest in even being aware of let alone addressing or sharing. About, if possible, learning to share them. Though it makes her uncomfortable, Chloe understands his urge to talk has less to do with happy-ever-afters than with the rooms and routines that come with them. Bill Disk advances a few such hopeful theories and Chloe, not unkindly, grows fitful. She is employee of the month and could be doing other things for a living.

Bill Disk has had lovers coming out of his ears. When one such lover had cold feet at an architecture conference in Montreal, he took off on his own and Marion had the same idea! When he stepped into the restaurant he had the sense of being at an appointment. They found themselves drinking fine Jurançon Sec and quickly checked into somewhere picture-postcard where she had to sleep in the bath because he snored like a chainsaw. They awoke and cried with excitement and cried over matters of the soul that even talk of moving in together immediately couldn't fix.

That night she can't sleep. For all that he haunts her, like a dead man, and for all her clarity, she cannot picture Joao. She finds photographs of their visit to his grandparents' almost uninhabitable house in the Algarve and considers his obsession about returning there and considers the agreeable but pointless notion of moving to Portugal. She thinks of fishing nets, piled up like pasta, and fishing boats, white and blue, the taste of cocaine from Joao's red-apple lips, and only when she sets fire to the photographs does she discover that she has wanted to talk to Bill Disk all along.

She checks on the lobby where she finds him alone by the drawing-room window, reading the previous day's *Irish Times*.

'Fancy randomly bumping into you here,' he says.

'I work here. This is not random. But it is a little early, no?'

'Is it?'

'And this is yesterday's paper?'

'I want to see what was in the news the day I got married.'

'That is a lovely idea,' says Chloe.

'And I don't know what else to do.'

'Excuse me?'

'I have known all along, or suspected at least, that I am destroying her life. I'd undo it all. If I could. Or reverse it.'

Chloe turns the colour of beef, looks at her feet and his, observes the bleary gleam of the river outside and slowly, stunned that she is doing so, says what she has been thinking all along.

'Are you sick?'

'I was. Cancer of the something. I'm clean now. You could serve breakfast on me. But that's why we're here. Because of the was.'

Thinking he was dying, Bill wanted the wedding to be something: a kind of settlement. He couldn't die without offering his devoted girlfriend something first, and he thought the wedding would help him find, if not a cure for the cancer, which eloquently cured itself, then at least the something missing neither of them could find once they had checked out of the hotel in Montreal.

'Without having any interest in making this any more significant than it has to be,' he says. 'I am now both not going to die and married to someone I don't love.'

Chloe sees the old fisherman walk down the path towards the jetty. He is taking his time, carrying a cool box that in the darkness resembles a bell. She can only look at the fisherman so long. There is absolutely no question of responding to Bill Disk's queries, of where she is from, what she plans to do when she leaves Ireland, what she dreams of, or who.

'I don't know,' she says.

Her thoughts on the matter, that, even as employee of the month, she is still defeated and out-thought by this country, do not make her want to go back to Nimes or follow

Joao to an inappropriate house in Portugal, another reason why she cannot answer Bill Disk's questions or return his gaze. Only then does it occur to her that she has already met his gaze, earlier, just then, the day before, when they first met.

Bill Disk goes for a walk by the river. Because guests expect to see her at breakfast she clears tables and resets them, making sure at least to create the illusion that she is not simply waiting for him to return. There is a call for her at reception and she arranges to meet him in a pub a mile from the hotel.

She orders a Fanta and waits for twenty, thirty minutes. Places like this mean very little to her. She supposes Bill Disk has returned to the bridal suite or perhaps he is on his way to the airport. Both bring on a kind of euphoria. It is like she was drowning and has escaped through the floor of the riverbed, only to drown again in an underwater ocean; which brings its own euphoria.

Bill Disk wanders in holding a cigar stub, a wayward but persistent look in his eyes.

'This is dried out. It's driftwood. Can I assume it won't be on my bill?'

She considers where they are and does not feel the need to reply. Soon her shift will be over. She offers to explain the situation to Marion Bishop.

'I suppose it's the least someone can do,' he says. They decide that Bill Disk will hide until Marion Bishop has gone

Marion Bishop is very calm. Not pleasant or particularly reasonable, but calm and committed to the situation, like a cop absorbing information, amassing it. Chloe says someone saw Bill Disk board a bus bound for Galway. This needs no explanation as far as Marion Bishop is concerned. She listens as if she has heard it all before. Chloe feels mysteriousness and mirth, as if all this has nothing to do with her.

She invites Marion Bishop to stay another night free of charge. She wonders about about what she will do if the offer is accepted, she wonders about the blank truth of a twelve-hour marriage, she wonders about doubt, the inescapable doubt that comes from successful relationships as well as failed ones. It's as if she has all the answers at the same time as not caring what they are. She watches Marion Bishop pack the last of her things, new bathing suits wrapped in tissue-paper, enormous necklaces wrapped in scarves. She walks Marion Bishop to the taxi, which she decides will be paid for by the hotel. At the car, they cordially discuss airlines and airports and she wonders what she can do with Bill Disk, now that the coast is clear. It is like she can fly the plane by just closing her eyes.

Bill Disk makes himself at home in Chloe's room. Expectations take hold of her, like pins and needles or a yawn, it is one thing to respect another's privacy but another altogether to be the centre of attention. She has never been in a situation like this, she loves the embarrassment, the drawn-out flush, as complicated as lacework.

She sits on the edge of the bed, and there, towards afternoon and evening, they have conversations that she can't quite understand, just like all the other things she can't understand. She does not want anything more to do with this man. She does not know what she was thinking. Bill Disk falls asleep with one of Joao's books open on his chest and she notices something and though she cannot quite tell where it has come in she sees that a bat is unhappily scrabbling around her room.

She waits a few moments before waking Bill Disk who puffs out of bed and throws whatever he can lay his hands on—cups, jewellery, a towel—at the frail and hysterical bat. A shoe hits Chloe in the face, Joao's gloves, clock and books fill the air. Bill Disk shrieks when the bat collides with him and Chloe stuffs wet tissues into the hole in the ceiling, not because she wants to divert any bats but because she is trying anything to make Bill Disk inaudible. His time is up.

'Did you get rid of my wife?' he says.

'Kaput,' says Chloe.

'Kaput? Kaput-kaput? I knew you were impressive but I didn't know you were an assassin. No offence, but let's go somewhere we can see some proper horses.'

Bill Disk's voice rings out and reverberates into nothing and not even aware that this is what she is doing, quietly she catches him by the arm and pulls him to the door where they stand until a silence tells her that the bat is gone and her bedroom is free from intruders but ruined.

Photo: Conor Friel

FEATURED POET

AILBHE DARCY grew up in Dublin, and has published poems in Ireland, Britain and the US. In 2010 she released a chapbook-length collection, *A Fictional Dress*, with tall-lighthouse press, and she is working towards a first collection, to be published by Bloodaxe Books. She co-edits *Moloch*, an online journal, and is a PhD student at the University of Notre Dame.

Socks

'The inherent unfinishedness and unpredictability of language—the fact that I can never deduce from any two of your words what the third one is going to be—is a token of human freedom, and thus in a broad sense political.'

—Terry Eagleton

I wear my socks odd, queer
bags a couple of feet from my

knees. I've heard that's how

the first dykes snagged the fair
sex: maybe some night I'll catch a feel.

Be honest, for that I wear my socks

spotted, freckled with eyes, crossed
all my t's as a young thing. I wear

my socks beneath my boots, where

they can't be seen. On very cold days
I wear my socks twice, and over my

tights, but always odd. I believe

that's right, the way you can't tell
what colour my knickers will be.

Shoes

for Muntazer al-Zaidi

Duck shoes! I saw them in a catalogue.
Not ugly waterproof kicks, or flippers
for me to flop about the deck on wet days,
or wear to the pond in the park. Not *duck, shoes.*
Nor shoes for a pet we might keep in a kennel,
it was late last night the duck was speaking of you,

But mallard heels in black, a duo of duckling heads
perched at one's toes, leather upper, insole, sole.
Designer Chie Mihara, decidedly retro, with a snap
closure strap looped round the ankle, €300 a pair,
not each. Duck shoes. For me! Come on, just think,

Just think of all the shoeless years! Those Cork stones
that rubbed a woman's sole to heck, the women still
barefooting it across Africa in search of a well,
and the years that were all too much about shoes,

Bound lotus feet, Marie Antoinette, Imelda Marcos.
Think of the spectacle! The bird-bodied celebrity
chicks who had everyone in thrall with their Blahniks,
and the nine-year-old girl who stepped with both
of her feet onto a land mine last week—

But not us! And so when we lay down in our double
bed last night it was duck shoes I didn't wear
to tramp all over your sleek white back,
trace with a toe the seam of your glammed-up cock,
raise my two legs like arms raised to cheer
over both of our grinning heads again, my dear.

Observations upon hearing she was leaving Australia

Her reports are all Web 2.0,
she is on the run.
A hall of mirrors such that
the source text is indeterminable.

*

She is keening today at a funeral for a stoat,
so she irons her red petticoat for a hood,
brushes her hair till it swoons, sets
her dandelion clock by the daytime moon,
all that jazz. Eats a hearty lunch, with wine,
pockets her black-handled knife, sets off,
her tale collected and catalogued.

*

On a blog about Britney:
So what if she lip-synchs?
The spectacle's the thing.

*

Holes for eyes cut in newspapers,
a full-length brown trenchcoat,
black, black Cadillac,
the shape of your heart.

*

I want to egg her on, set her
going like a flat black clock
with a MIDI alarm. But perhaps
she knows something radial and whole.

*

Bones stacked, her body falls
into an unswerving column—
ears, shoulders, hips, ankles.

Buttocks relaxed, legs back,
belly strong, head raised.
She imagines someone pulls

a string from the back
of her head, allowing her chin
to fall level and her throat

to soften. She does not tuck
her tailbone. That's what I
imagine.

*

Just as my phone lights up with her
position, my battery's dead.
I'm left with a memory
of what she might have said.

*

Singing: How does an ant
work out how far it is back

to the nest? Glue stilts to its legs
before it strides out to the wilds;

take them off and it will walk
only part of the way back.

Does someone go out and collect
the ants after the experiment is over?

*

Something like:
knowledge is diasporic,
do not pass Go.

Ailbhe Darcy

A Report from the Mapparium, Boston

Between the trapeze and your feet,
for the sake of argument, we'll write it so,
there must have been a space where she was solitary

before she dropped. I read once how a woman
died in plastic surgery, hankering after
the more herself. Frightened, perhaps, of solitary,

she can't have dreamed how her husband
would push the heels of his hands hard
against his eyes at night when he was solitary

hoping to catch sight of her moving face
he's losing, or his eyes to bleed. Whisper at one end,
the child at the other hears as if you both were solitary

and telling the secretest things. The sound
travels up and over. But stand in the middle
and you sound surround sound, utterly solitary.

Too, the drummer in a band I loved and never
met has died in his sleep at thirty-four, for no
good reason. Each of these events is solitary.

Well I'm not gay, but he won me over, I'd sing
at his funeral. Now I turn to Jay sometimes and try
to breathe: night with or without him is solitary.

Elsewhere I read how Edison would hold a steel
ball in either hand as he considered these things.
If he fell to sleep, a ball, a solitary

ball would drop and he'd awake. Whatever came
unto his mind just then, that was the answer
to the question, a kind of Solitaire.

Ailbhe Darcy

The Monster Surely

January, and the monster is still wearing your spectacles.
I have to read the daily specials to you from blackboards.

I want to ask you why you gave your spectacles to a monster.
But instead you get down on one knee and ask me to marry you.

Monstrous, his marshy breath steaming up your expensive spectacles.
I answer an ad for an eight-month-old coonhound.

That monster, I mutter, is pure spectacle for the neighbours.
And you can't walk the dog because you can't read the signposts.

I start waking at night to read the monster Ginsberg:
O monster for real feed my hunger for spectacle:
and fall for myself, in your huge monstrous spectacles.

Toes

Okay. I was no friend to you
in those years, the years
before you left. I kept you
on your toes, though. In
his memoir, Tobias Wolff
says: 'Isn't there, in the very
act of confession, an obscene
self-congratulation for
the virtue required to see
your mistake and own up…?'
I imagine a pause and a cough.
The audience do not know
where to put their feet. The water's
rising. Perhaps they raise their hands,
or go out back for a smoke. I want
to call you, but know you may hang up.

Ailbhe Darcy

Watching

I watched them again this morning.
I borrowed my father's glass, the one that extends,
and I cut a forked branch from the forest
to steady my arm and keep the image clear.
The boy, the dirty one, brought wild birds' eggs and weeds in from the forest.
When he gave them to the woman, she took them from him
and she offered him her hands, holding them in front of her
open wide like a blessing. And he walked into her embrace.
They have cats now in their house, in every room.
They keep all their kittens. They drown none of them.
They walk on the beds, on the breakfast table, they feed the cats their food.
I saw the dirty boy kissing a kitten. It sickened me to see it.
He was hugging it, holding it closely against his skin inside his shirt.
When the man came home from the fields, the woman filled a tin bath with hot water
and she washed him. He was naked. She poured the water over him,
she soaped his hair, she washed him down and down,
she was doing things to him that made me feel strange.
After, they went up to the bedroom and they lay on the bed.
I can't describe what they did. It was sorcery, I am sure of that.
I wanted to get father's gun and run over and kill them.
They are wicked people. That's what father says.
So. Now I will watch and watch and note and miss nothing
and I will gather in the proof and then I will tell.
And they will burn.

Tom Cleary

One Owner Only

John Kenny

He is sitting in his Twin Cam.

The engine is ticking over and the booster fan on. Full heat, and arrow at the head of the white matchstick man. The windows might soon fog because the controls aren't right, but he has had his last look on town in the early morning air so the windows stay up. Shut.

He rolls the seat back from the wheel and springs off the belt. The headrest is no ease so he turns and kneels back sharp and tears it from its sockets. It's a faceless creature with two notched legs, and he stands it as a passenger to the side in the seat.

Jersey off, and his browned arms are strong in the sawn-off T-shirt. He fist-slaps his knees and turns up his grimed hands looking at each in turn. Clenches, flexes, then motions outwards to catch a slow ball.

Gone. Clean through his hands.

Eyes widened then shut, he grabs fists of his hair and pulls his head down into his chest till he rocks back and forth, first like going to sleep but then faster and faster winding up.

He finally stops, and stops grinding his teeth and the grinding sound in his throat and stretches back up. Eyes wider again, he rolls the seat forward and sits down straight.

Clutched, he feels the bone-joint sound of the stick through the gears. Looks down for some sense in the lines between numbers. Think. First. Second. Third. Keep going. Fourth. Fifth. Think.

Neutral.

Handbrake off. Pedals set underfoot. He reaches for the roof and clicks off the little interior light.

More visible now as it brightens, along the pier there is still only him to think the speed in this thing you should see her go.

*

They had started into the digging not long after they bought it.

James had sold his old two-door for parts and bought his turbo diesel '00 reg and there was no way too much time would go by now before Noel would have to do the same.

James was for the inner details, but for Noel all depended only on the look, so when they spotted the ad in the paper all Noel could see was sleek silver metal over thick black tyres while James went through the given specs and made approving judgments about mileage and model resale value.

Alloy wheels. Front and back spoilers. Remote CD changer. Clean, reliable. Will accept nearest offer…

A quick mobile call, a trip to the Credit Union, and this morning they were wrapped safe in the blare of James's five-door-speaker stereo on the way to do the business.

Pulling out after a quick Supermac's meal deal halfway there, James told Noel to pull out the map and see if he could find the small hole that somehow had a decent man with a decent secondhand for sale.

But after the first turn off the main road the directions somehow went skewed, so when they saw her thumbing they said they'd throw her a lift and she'd maybe set them back right the same time.

Hard to tell what age, but she hopped in lively, hardly waiting for the ask when they'd stopped.

No, she wasn't afraid of thumbing these days, day nor night nor anytime. Far? She'd tell them when she knew she was there. You know yourself she said and stuck her head out from the back, looked them right and left in the eyes.

She was wearing the white blouse of a waitress, with a name tag too faded to read. She was just coming off a twelve-hour shift she said, but when they pushed her for more they got none, and she sat with her arms laid over the backseat like she was with them all day for the trip.

They looked at each other quick and James slowed.

Hang on now. Stall it all here a minute.

Give it to her.

When Noel moved to turn around he was near afraid of interrupting her humming, but he handed back the ad page to see. She took the map and his elbow, and keep going along here she said, then there and then there.

Great. That's great.

Off again.

Faster now from the help, James said she should give them her number, there might always be a next time.

No. And her head came forward again. But why don't both of you give me yours?

There wasn't much talk after that and they let her off at a forestry scheme where she said. All they did was look as she went straight across the road to the trees.

What do you say to that?

Not long after they let her off, they pulled into a large yard at the end of a byroad pointed out finally by a strolling old couple who had a good gawk at the pair of them sitting within in the noise and a good shake of the head at the cut of the car. The exhaust left them for dust.

Along a line of revamps, Noel spotted it quick. And could picture it alright as he circled. Could see all this silver and black and himself, cruising. That designer interior behind his reflection in the windshield would be something at weekends.

Mick Giblin of Midland Motors had come hand-rubbing Swarfega out of a galvanised shed at the back of the yard and was already head to head with James. After a quick test run there was a thumbs-up all round and Mick Giblin was sticking twenty for luck in Noel's shirt pocket.

True lover of bypasses, James led them on the way home onto the best acceleration stretches, and they got into town as it darkened to do three or four dual circuits of the square.

Noise it up.

This town. This town knows above ever they're alive.

They finished off along the pier before pints, with James rolling the first of a new grass stash and repeating his gospel of the day. It was time for Noel to get moving now this was sitting under him. He would have to learn to do his own improvements. Get up to speed.

There was only one thing for it. He would have to dig his own pit.

Then in for the retelling of the mighty many ways of going bloody astray. Fame and shoulder-punches and a round of shorts. Daft. Hard to say what she looked like. A royal midlands tour, hah? Middle of nowhere and she was gone.

Tell us again.

And the day got bigger each time.

They decided anew on their favourite fundamentals in the course of the digging.

James took a long weekend from the joinery and came round early to Noel's despite the Thursday night half-spree, set on hitting the tone for the day ahead as he hand-braked in round the back of the house driving the cattle mad away from the fence with his fanfare horn.

Noel's father had soundly given the go-ahead for the conversion of the old cart-house at the far end of the track down to Rafftery's field, and Noel had already made a quick rough box in there dragging an old harrow pin along the packed surface clay.

But walking across this now, James sent Noel off to finish his morning jobs and took in from his boot his old surveyor's tape and powder reel. Just about smiling at Noel's skewed eye, he made his own calculations. And then he chalked the lines. Slow and clean and solid.

Then they were soon moving. And they went from one known area of talk to another without much disagreement as the work went on.

Didn't matter how often they took off early twice a week for a half-hour's puck-about before training so long as they reached the quarter-finals at least.

Nothing short of a miracle that Joanne had agreed to go out with James in the first place. Let alone to have agreed to engage him once her four years were put down now at uni.

If you got hitched up you'd have to steady up a bit.

Whatever happened with anything you'd always need to know the shape of things quick.

Hell with the panic anyhow.

Stay put. Keep the head down.

No. Kick away into the action plan. Take off.

Out of town. The country.

Or finish it.

One way or the other just go. Go.

Right.

Shovel, pick, spade and barrow took them late that day into the ground, a hole two men long, man and a half wide, one man deep.

It took almost the full following day to do the concrete floor and the blocks up the sides and fit it out with a few racks and stands for all the tools James had made Noel buy at the Traveller market.

Now that's some pit.

You could live down there. Settle in.

By evening, when they backed the car in over and James had given Noel a few quick pointers down underneath, they were thirsty with achievement. As ready for the night as if they'd been taking their ease.

Joanne had made it home out of the blue just for the night. She'd some friend or other with her and there might be something there for Noel. Friday and Saturday night would be rolled sure into one.

They took both cars.

Noel filled her up on the way in and put down the time it would take James to get out to Joanne's home place and back by practising his handbrake turn in the car park out at the pitch.

Then flat to the mat into town.

He parked just off the square, in tight between some sort of old camper van and a beaut of a Merc Sports.

Through the lounge in O'Connell's, down to the proper bar at the back.

A pint.

James and Joanne and this friend of hers were taking their time alright.

His second pint tasted like his pure worth as he set it down and elbowed in to take the cue and chalk up and break for his turn.

He cleared as ever table after table. Finished a last quick black before handing his win to the next up when James finally stuck the head in and signaled him drinks in hand towards the front. Up at the bar there, Joanne was whispering into the ear of a honey done up in all pinks and whites and killer jeans.

After Noel welcomed Joanne home and she'd quickly done the hellos he was left to his own devices with Nicola. She was all talk. Even took him to the side by the hand. A lot of questions without much wait for the answers Noel began to want to give.

He was wondering about James and Joanne over on their own in the side snug when Nicola moved for the bar and told him to have another.

Just the one so.

But when he looked back from studying the day's match results on the corner telly Joanne and Nicola were coming at him at the same time. All he got from Joanne was bye Noel as he was shoved his pint and the girls tugged one another out the door.

Barely a chance to sit before James stopped his stare in his glass, downed it and stood.

C'mon. Put yours in you quick. Have you your keys? Go up for a few cans. Time we saw what she can really do.

They only started racing when they'd gone beyond the lights to dark but known roads.

More pints later would help fill in the story, so time enough. Lash into the cans for now.

They pulled up alongside and yelled across through their rolled-down windows. Gave those stereos volume.

Belted along grand for a bit.

Then he got in front.

He hit a mock emergency stop. Took a small tip on the back bumper.

He roared ahead again.

He caught up. Pulled ahead on a bend and gave him the full fog-lights back into the face.

Catch up. Quick.

Fast. Open her up.

And he rammed ahead for one last time. And he saw the lights go in rearview.

Reverse.

God God.

Hit reverse.

Never be fast enough. So he swung round sharp in the next gap.

He had seen it as a simple sailing in over a soft-margined low ditch and almost missed the spot going back. He faced his lights in, and now he fell and ran through rushes and seepage and slipped out onto tyre tears on newly cut grass to where after whatever number of turns the car showed off to any looker only a steaming damaged belly and reflected in what of its windows was left only the night sky.

When he sees him twisted half in and half out of the windscreen he knows straight away it's all done. He thinks he can't but he can and he checks anyhow, unwinds arms and legs and drags him out, lies him down and tries for the heart and the breath. Does the chest with his hands, tries again and again until he can hear himself shouting.

Then grabs out his mobile.

But ring who?

On his knees, he looks down long at the closed eyes and hears now louder as if they're happening the chats upon chats rounded off in handshakes.

And another sound comes through. How the hell can an upturned smashed engine still be running?

He is shook beyond himself.

This is what?

Like sober and stocious at once.

Count to yourself. Count.

Do something. Tell no one. Yet anyhow. Do something yourself.

Do what?

However long he would sit all he would ever see or hold here was blood and bone and glass, and skewed coloured metal that looked thin enough to mould back into shape in the hands.

This is where?

No sound now almost. No passing lights.

He is sitting down in the dark.

He has driven here straight, left it all back there behind.

When he climbed down into the pit first he stood, ready to fix all round him, but when he drank the last can he stopped his quick pace end to end, and sank.

Sit. Steady now. Stop the speeding head.

Smell of clay and oil and drying concrete under the old rib-rafters he can see now with the strong new inspection lamp in his hand. On and off with the lamp for a long time up out of the ground, a signaling surely for other lights that will soon come.

Sit down here and wait. See what comes.

Sit.

But soon he points the lamp slow along the pit walls and stands up.

All the tools lie there lovely, look at them, laid in order in rows, and he moves his hand along them.

He takes up a spanner and turns it around in the light. He thumbs the adjustment one way, then the other. Drops it and picks up another. And another. Then ratchets, hacksaw, combination wrenches. Throws some. Lets others fall. Angle grinder. Lump hammer. Socket sets size by size, extension bars, hex keys, grip-pliers.

Finally he climbs out and looks at it all dropped shining in a heap down there. All that chrome.

He drags the lamp on its stand to hang down along the edge.

On or off or smash it?

Outside, the night is near gone, so just go.

Go and have a last look at town.

Go.

He sits in. Starts and turns her for town. Then revving her up to the last he takes off back along the track a lot less quietly than he'd come.

Reaching You

The horizon tilts
as the plane turns, descends.
My ears block,
the chewing gum, useless as always,
stretches between my frantic teeth.
We land in the rain,
bouncing,
slowing,
stopping.

Four hours later
my ears pop,
my headache recedes,
but by then I am in bed beside you,
your saliva still drying
on my skin.

Edward Lee

Things I See

Mary Costello

Outside my room the wind whistles. It blows down behind our row of houses, past all the bedroom windows and when I try to imagine the other bedrooms and the other husbands and wives inside I hear my own husband moving about downstairs. He will have finished reading the paper by now and will have broken up the chunks of burning coal in the grate. Then he will carry the tray into the kitchen, walking slowly, with the newspaper folded under his arm. He will wash up the mugs and leave them to drain; he will flip up the blind so that the kitchen will be bright in the morning. Finally, he will flick off the socket switches and gather up his bundle of keys. Occasionally, just, he will pause and make himself a pot of tea to have at the kitchen table, the house silent around him. As he moves I follow him from above. I know the way he sits at the table, his long legs off to the side, the paper propped against the teapot, or staring into the corner near the back door, pensive. He drinks his tea in large mouthfuls and gives the mug a discreet little lick, a flick of the tongue, to prevent a drip. When I hear his chair scrape the tiles I switch off my lamp and turn over. Don is predictable and safe. Tonight he is making himself that last pot of tea.

There are nights when I want to go down and shadow him and stand behind his chair and touch his shoulders. My long pale arms would wind around his neck and I would lean down so that our faces touch. Some nights between waking and sleeping I dream that I do this but I stand and watch him from the kitchen door and I am aware only of the cold of the tiles under my bare feet. There is something severe and imperious in Don's bearing that makes me resist. He has a straight back and square shoulders and black black hair. His skin is smooth and clear, without blemish, as if he has many layers of perfect epidermii. Beside him, with my pale skin and fair hair I am like an insignificant underground animal, looking out at him through weak eyes.

Lucy, my sister, is staying with us for a week. She is sleeping in the next room and sometimes I hear the headboard knock against the wall as she tosses. I get up and stand at the window. The light from the kitchen illuminates the back garden and the gravel path down to the shed. If I peer out I can see the ivy on the back wall. When I am away from this house I have to let my mind spill over into this room before I can sleep. I have to reconstruct it in the strange darkness of another room before I can surrender. Its window bears onto the old fir trees looming tall and dark beyond our back wall. There is the house and these trees and a patch of sky above and these borders keep me penned in and I like this. I cannot face large vistas, long perspectives, lengthy hopes. When we first came here Don wanted us to take the front room; it is west-facing and bright and looks onto the street. He likes to hear the sounds of the neighbourhood; he likes to know there are lives going on around us. Some nights he sleeps out there. This evening he told me I was intolerant.

Tonight I wish I could be alone in the house. I would walk around the carpeted rooms upstairs, straightening curtains, folding clothes, arranging things. I would lie on the bed and inhale Don's cool scent on the pillow, hours after he has slept there and this contact, this proximity to him, would be enough to make me nervous and excitable, make my thoughts too hopeful. Sometimes when Don and Robin are away from me and I am alone in the house I am prone to elation, prone to being swept up in some vague contentment at the near memory of them. I let myself linger in their afterglow, and then something—a knock on the door, a news item on the TV, the gas boiler firing up outside—will shatter it all. Lately when I am alone I become concerned for our future. It is not the fact of growing old, but of growing different. Don becomes impatient if I say these things and I see his face change and I know he is thinking, For God's sake, woman, pull yourself together.

I go into the bathroom and the light stings my eyes. I splash water on my face. He will hear my movements now. I rub on cream and massage the skin around my eyes and cheek bones. My eyes are blue, like Lucy's. There are four girls in my family and we all have blue eyes. I go out on the landing and lean over the banisters and see the line of light under the kitchen door. I pause outside Lucy's door. I imagine her beneath the bedclothes, the sheet draped over her shoulders, her hair spilling onto the pillow. Lucy is a musician; she plays the cello in an orchestra and this evening she played a Romanian folk dance in the living room. Robin was in her jammies, ready for bed and afterwards she picked up Lucy's bow. Lucy let her turn it over carefully and explained about horsehair and rosin and how string instruments make music and she showed her how to pluck a string. Then she whisked her up into her arms and nuzzled her and breathed in my daughter's apple-scented hair.

'Have you thought about music lessons for her?' she asked me a moment later. 'She could learn piano, or violin. She's old enough, you know.' Before I could reply she brought her face close to Robin's. 'Would you like that, Sweetheart, would you like to play some real mew-sic?' Robin giggled and clung to Lucy like a young monkey. They sat on the sofa together and I smiled across at Robin. A bluebottle came from nowhere in November and buzzed around the room.

'I don't know,' I said. 'She's already got so much going on. And she's only six.' I watched the bluebottle zigzag drunkenly above the up-lighter and for a second I was charged with worry. Every day insects fly into that lighted corner and land on the halogen bulb and extinguish themselves in a breath.

'Don't leave it too late, Annie. She's got an ear, she's definitely got an ear. I said so to Don today.'

She carried Robin upstairs then and they left a little scent in their wake. It reminded me of the cream roses that clung to the arched trellis in our garden at home. No, it reminded me of Lucy. I think she has always given off this scent, like she's discarding a surfeit of love. I wonder if all that wood and rosin and sheep gut suffocates her scent. I think of her sitting among the other cellists, her bulky instrument leaning back between her knees, her hair falling on one side of her face, the bow in her right hand drawing out each long mournful note, the fingers of her left hand pressed on the neck of the instrument or sliding down the fingerboard until I think she will bleed out onto the strings. I watched those hands today as they passed Robin a vase of flowers. She has taught Robin to carry the flowers from room to room as we move.

I turn and tiptoe into Robin's room. The lamp light casts a glow on her skin and her breathing is silent and for a moment I am worried and think to hold a tiny mirror to her mouth, the way nurses check the breath of the dying. She is a beautiful child, still and contained and perfect, and so apart from me that sometimes I think she is not mine, no part of me claims her. Don has stayed home and is raising her mostly and she is growing confident. Often at work I pause midway through typing a sentence, suddenly reminded of them, and I imagine them at some part of their day: Don making her lunch, talking to her teacher, clutching her schoolbag and pausing to wait up for her along the footpath. I have an endless set of images I can call on. This evening as I pulled into the drive Don was putting his key in the door. The three of them, Don, Lucy and Robin had been for a walk. It was windy, they had scarves and gloves on and their cheeks were flushed. Lucy and Robin laughed and waved at me as I pulled in. I sat looking at them all for a moment. Now I have a new image to call on.

If I ever have another child I will claim it—I will look up at Don after the birth and say, 'This one's mine.' I have it all planned.

After dinner this evening Don took the cold-water tap off the kitchen sink. He spread newspapers and tools all over the floor and cleared the shelves and stretched into the cupboard to work on the pipes. He opened the back door and went out to the shed and back several times and cold air blew through the house. After a while there was a gurgle, a gasp and a rush of water spilled out along the shelf onto the floor. He jumped back and cursed. Robin was in the living room watching Nickelodeon and Lucy was practising in the dining room. I had been roaming about the house tidying up, closing curtains, browsing. I had stepped over Don a few times and over the toolbox and spanners and boxes of detergent strewn around him.

'What's up?' I asked finally. His head was in the cupboard. 'What are you at?' I pressed.

'Freeing it up,' he said, and I thought of the journey his words had to make, bouncing off the base of the sink before ricocheting back out to me. 'Didn't you notice how slow it's been lately?'

I leaned against the counter. The sound of the cello drifted in from the next room, three or four low-pitched notes, a pause, then the same notes repeated again.

'Wouldn't the plunger have cleared it?' I said this so low that he might not have heard me above the notes. I viewed his long strong torso half-twisted and his shoulders pressing painfully against the edge of the bottom shelf. He drew up one leg as he strained to turn a bolt. His brown corduroys were threadbare at the knee and the sight of it made me almost forgive him. The cello paused and then started again and I focused on the notes, and tried to recognise the melody. Lucy favours Schubert; she tells me he is beyond purity. I have no ear and can scarcely recognise Bach.

'Is that urgent?' I asked.

'Nope.'

'Can't it wait then?'

I sensed his slow blink. Next door I heard Lucy turn over a page, sensed her pause, sigh and steady herself before raising her bow. A single sombre note began to unfurl into the surrounding silence and when I thought it could go on no longer and she really would bleed out of her beautiful hands, it touched the next one and ascended and then descended the octave and I thought this is Bach, this is that sublime suite that we listened to over and over in the early months of the pregnancy, and then never again, because Don worried that such melancholy would affect his unborn child.

'Can't you do these jobs during the day, when there's no one about?' I blurted. A new bar had begun and the music began to climb, began to envelop again.

He reversed out of the cupboard and threw the spanner in the box. 'What the hell is needling you this evening?'

'Shh. Keep your voice down. Please.' It was Bach, and I strove to catch each note and draw out the title while I still could, before it closed in.

He started to gather up the scattered tools and throw them in the toolbox. 'Jesus, Ann, we have to live. This is a house, a home… not some kind of mausoleum.' I sat there half listening. The music began to fade until only the last merciful note lingered. I can recognise the signs, the narrowing of his eyes as he speaks, the sourness of his mouth, when he's hurt and abhorred and can no longer stand me, and when the music stopped I wanted to stop this too, send him a message.

He leaned towards me then and spoke in a low tight voice. 'Everything has to be your way, doesn't it? Jesus, Ann, why are you so fucking intolerant?'

He slumped against the sink and stared hard at me so that I had to avert my eyes and seek out the darkness beyond the window. I felt Lucy's attempt to muffle our anger with the shuffle of her sheet music and cello and stand. I longed for her to start up again, send out a body of sound that would enrapture, and then I wondered if he had heard it, if it had reached him under the sink all this time, and if he'd remembered or recognized or known it. What was that piece, I longed to ask him, that sonata that Lucy played just now, the one we once loved, you and I?

'Look at you now, Ann. Do you know what you're doing?'

I thought of them, Lucy, Robin and Don at the front door earlier and the lawn spread itself before me again. The three of them had been laughing. Who was it who had said something funny? Robin is sallow like her father, with long dark hair and some strands had blown loose from her scarf. Don was laughing too but when he saw my car he averted his eyes and singled out the key in his bundle. There was a look on his face. I have seen that look before. It is a dark downcast look and when he looked away this evening perhaps he was remembering another day, the day that I was remembering too.

Robin was newly born and Lucy had come to stay for a few weeks after finishing college, to relieve us at times with Robin. I had wanted a child for a long time and now, when I recall them, I think those early days were lived in a strange surreal blur. At night, unable to sleep, I would turn and look at Don in the warmth of the night-light, his dark features made patient and silent by sleep, and I would think how I wanted to preserve us—Don, Robin and me—forever in the present then, in this beautiful amber glow.

I had gone into the city that day and had walked about the parks and the streets and the shops watching my happy face slide from window to window. Giddy, I bought a packet of cigarettes and sat outside a café and watched people's faces and felt a surge of hope. An old couple came out with their tray and sat down, reticent, but content. Young girls crowded around tables, self-consciously flicked their long hair and chatted to boys. I lit a cigarette and broke off half of the chocolate that came with my coffee and nibbled it, saving the rest for later, to disguise the cigarette smoke on my breath. I had not smoked for years and the cold air and the deep draw spiked my lungs and the surge of nicotine quickened my heartbeat and made my fingers tremble and I closed my eyes and slid into the drunkenness of it all.

Suddenly I was startled by a pigeon brushing past my arm and landing at my feet. It fluttered and hopped awkwardly on one leg and I saw the damaged foot on the other leg. There remained only one misshapen toe with an ingrown nail coiled tightly around it, swollen, sore, unusable. I met the pigeon's round, black, empty eye and thought of the word derelict and suddenly it seemed like the saddest word I had ever encountered. Two more pigeons landed close by and pecked at fallen crumbs. And then a gust of wind—tight against the street—came from nowhere and tossed napkins and paper cups and wrappers from the tables. My chocolate, half eaten in its gold-foil wrapper, blew to the ground. My pigeon hopped over and pecked at it and I smiled at his good fortune and then, in anxiety, thought that Don would now smell the cigarette when I got home. I glanced at my watch in panic and remembered Robin and her tiny clenched baby fists and her moist eyelids, and wondered why I had ever left her. I went to rise and a terrible racket of flapping wings and screeching occurred at my feet where the other pigeons had come for the chocolate and cornered my lame one. 'Shoo, Shoo,' I called at them but it came out as a whisper. I waved my arms and tried to rise again but with my loud heart and my shaking hands and the terrible screeching of pigeons I fell back into the chair.

Later I fled the city, trembling, and drove quickly towards the suburbs, with Robin on my mind and an odd fear that I might not see her again.

At the front door I reached into my pockets but found no key. I looked in the living-room window. Robin was asleep in her Moses crib. She was there, safe, and she was mine.

I walked around to the back of the house. The old fir trees appeared to be pressed flat against the sky and everything was still. The neighbourhood was silent and the birds and the dogs and the children's street-play were all absent, or that is how I remember it, as if all living creatures had sensed danger and fled, like they do on high Himalayan or Alpine ground before an avalanche. The back door is half glass and Don had his back to me. I raised my hand to knock on the glass and then I saw Lucy, in front of him, wedged up against the counter. He stood over her, leaning into her, with an arm each side of her and his palms flat on the counter. He was spread-eagled; he had her cornered. Her body and face were hidden from me; her hands moved on his shoulders, pressing them, and then her slender fingers touched his neck and traced the outline of his face, and her legs, in jeans, emerged from between his. I looked at the back of his head, at his thick black hair, his square shoulders. He was wearing a check shirt I had given him at Christmas, and his dark brown corduroy trousers. He moved his hips and his thighs and I thought: she is too small for him, he will crush her. But I underestimate Lucy.

And then he stopped moving and tilted his head, as if hearing something. He turned his face to the right and I slid back. All he would have seen was a shadow, like a bird's, cross the back door. I walked lightly to the front and leaned against the window. Later I rang the doorbell and pretended to search for something in the boot. And things started to come out and move again. A car drove into the cul-de-sac and a child yelped and lifted his tricycle up onto the footpath. An alarm went off at the other end of the road. Finally Don opened the door.

'I forgot my keys,' I explained quickly. He looked at me, that too calm unquiet look.

'You should have come around the back. Robin might have woken with the bell.'

'Did she sleep the whole time?' I asked and we looked at each other for a terrible moment and neither one of us heard his reply.

Now I hear his movements below and I become anxious. He is opening the back door. Does he, Don, step outside and gaze at the stars on nights like this? Does he stand under that dome of darkness and wonder at it all, at the waxing and the waning of the moon, the black silence? I have a strange sense of being in both places—down below with him and here in the bed. My heart is thumping and I am agitated and far from sleep now.

Suddenly I am exhausted from the effort of tracking him below. I am restless and my bed is too warm, too familiar, like a sickbed. I move and try to use up all the space and lie horizontally and remember a childhood illness, a fever in my darkened room, and my mother's voice saving me. And now I want Don here, I want the memory of him here. I want him beside me so that I can find the slope of his body against which to lie. I want him to reach across the wide bed and draw me into his arms. I want him to lay his large hand flat on my belly and press softly and feel desire flood though me. I want to be silent and dreamy and see this room, the treetops, everything, from a different angle. I want to be shielded by trees and forget everything and lie against him and sleep.

'You asleep?'

I did not hear him come upstairs. He has stolen upon me before I am prepared. He approaches my side of the bed but stands back a little. Though my eyes are closed I can feel the distance. His voice is soft and defeated. I open my eyes and look at him. I am waiting for some sound from within, searching for a few syllables to knit into words that will not disappoint, just a few, to send across this small space and call him. He waits too and a long look passes between us and I know something has been spoilt, and then he moves away and starts to undress. And for the first time his undressing, piece by piece, is too intimate and crushing and revealing and I close my eyes and weep.

He goes into the bathroom and shuts the door. In a moment I hear the flush and the brushing of teeth. When he returns he walks around the room and hangs up his clothes, unplugs the hairdryer, puts his shoes away. Now and then he clears his throat in a precise, emphatic way. He does this when we argue—he appears occupied in his task, untouched, untroubled, aloof. He does it to distance me, to reduce me, to make me think *this is nothing*. And I am left wondering—do I magnify everything, do I magnify the words and the pain and the silences? Do I?

He reaches for a pillow and for a moment I think he is going to take it to the front room. But he gets in beside me. The lamp is still on by his side. He is sitting there with his arms folded, looking from him and I can feel the rise and fall of his chest. I wonder at his thoughts, at those clear thoughts I imbue him with, at his certainty, at how he seeks always to unscramble things when all I can summon is silence and how I will never know him but always imagine him. Outside I hear the occasional flapping of our clothes on the clothesline and the faint distant whistle of the wind, as if it has moved off and left our house alone tonight. And I think this is how things are, and this is how they will remain, and with every new night and every new wind I know that I am cornered too, and I will remain, because I cannot unlove him.

Sliocht as Turas na mBolcán

Brollach

Dhá thaibhreamh
Roimh chur chun farraige—
Bloc gallúnaí a d'fhás is a d'fhás
Faoi mo charball.
Leis sin féin, an dara mír—
Doirseoir óstáin ag láimhseáil pinn.
Leaba is bia gan iarraidh fós,
Bhris sé ubh de bharr mo chinn.
Chuireas an seomra in áirithe, air sin
Is suas liom an staighre in airde:
Gúna dúnadh thiar,
Folt dorcha, gealacán is buí.

Teacht Isteach

(I)

Déanann siad—na daoine—
Dealbha as laibhe an tsléibhe.
De bharr an teasa ina gcré,
Ní fiú faic a saothar.
Súil ná béal, ní mhaisíonn
A dtairiscintí dearga,
Ach dhá chíoch ar bhean
Is ar an bhfear, ball fearga.
Ní ciotach ann mé a thuilleadh,
Nuair a thugaim dá n-earraí diúltú—
Lámha riastacha an oileáin,
Ní féidir iad a chúiteamh.

An Chéad Fhear

(II)

Giolla ospidéil ab ea fear amháin
Go ndeachaigh sé i mblianta—
Gan tógáil othair ann níos mó
Is lomairt na leapa á gciapadh.
Siúlann sé is siúlann leis,
Gan neach ar cheachtar taobh de,
Scaipeann samhnas béil na hoíche,
Gáire calcaithe na teilifíse.
Ach fiafraigh fios an bhealaigh de,
Labhróidh glór dorchla lán cruinnis
Éide chruthanta arís é—
Is é an post an duine.

Aifric Mac Aodha

Excerpt from Journey to the Volcano

Introduction

Two dreams
before setting out on my journey—
a block of soap which grew and grew
Beneath the roof of my mouth.
Then the second scene—
a hotel porter behind a desk,
Neither bed nor board booked,
he cracks an egg over my head.
I make my reservation,
And climb the staircase:
a dress that fastens at the back,
dark hair, egg white and yolk.

First Days

(I)

And they, the natives, mold
figurines from mountain lava.
But since the clay's too hot,
Their work lacks refinement.
Eyes, or a mouth, don't enhance
their molten red statues,
but two breasts on the female
and on the male, a penis.
I am not awkward anymore
when I refuse their wares—
those raw hands of the island,
that will never be repaid.

The First Man

(II)

This man here was once an orderly
until he got too old himself,
He couldn't turn the bedsore
Patients, or tend to their aches.
He walks and walks, with no one there,
on either side of him. By now, he's cast
Off some of the night-time sickness—
the petrified laughter of televisions.
But stop and ask him for directions,
he'll answer in a corridor voice.
He's back in uniform again—
A person is his role.

Translated by Denise Blake

Echtrae Conlae

do Keara Killian

Dhá scéal a rachadh faoin gcroí: Echtrae Conlae agus 'Eveline' Joyce.
Feic 'Eveline', ar dtús: Í suite ag an bhfuinneog agus an tsráid á feistiú le cuimhní cinn a hóige.
Tá cuireadh faighte aici éalú le fear farraige agus is í atá idir dhá chomhairle.
Eveline, ní imeoidh.
Ná bímís soineanta faoin scéal, ach go háirithe: ní haon dualgas iníne a choinníonn siar í
ach tarraingt an ghnáthaimh.
Ionann scéal d'Eveline agus do Chonlae (.i. leannán, bád is cuireadh chun imeachta),
ach amháin seo—go ngéilleann an t-óglach.
Is é an cathú dochloíte é, a shamhlú conas a bhí aige féin is ag bean a mheallta, ón uair gur chuireadar
chun farraige is gur imíodar leo, dá naomhóg ghloine, ghreanta.

Labhraíonn Conlae:

Domsa, níorbh éasca:
Ó thosach go deireadh báid liom,
Ó dheireadh go tosach,
Ba chorrach ar mo dhá chos mé.

Ní cláir adhmaid a bhí fúm,
Ach cláir ghloine:
Ní bean a bhí faram
Ach míle scáil i mo choinne.

Dar liom go raibh an t-uisce féin
Á shiúl agam—
Is níor le háthas é
Ach le teann míshuaimhnis.

Trí aoibhneas a choill sí orm:
Lúth ar thalamh,
Bean gan aithne,
Machaire balbh.

Aifric Mac Aodha

The Adventure of Conlae

for Keara Killian

Two stories unsettle my heart: The Adventure of Conlae and Joyce's 'Eveline'.
Take Eveline first, sitting by her window. The street is being drawn in by childhood memories.
She has an offer to escape across the ocean with a sailor but she is caught between the two worlds.
Eveline? She didn't go.
Let's not be naïve about it either: she's is not held there by a daughter's sense of duty so much as by the appeal of all that's safe and un-new to her.
Eveline and Conlae have a similar story (a lover, a boat and an invitation to escape), but the difference is—the young man yielded.
The temptation is to try and imagine Conlae with his enchantress from the first moment they took to sea in the strange glass boat.

Conlae Speaks:
For me, it was never painless:
From stern to prow
And back again
My feet gave under me.

I didn't have wooden boards under me
but a boat made of glass.
I didn't have a woman beside me
but a thousand shadows on every side.

It felt like I had begun
to walk on water
and it didn't give me peace
but a strange sense of unease.

She took three things away from me:
the power to move my legs on land,
the allure of an unknown woman,
the stillness of the ground.

translated by Denise Blake

One of us

The good looking, charming man Margaret
always had a soft spot for, pinstripe smoothie
Cecil, with his boyish smile, brylcremed hair,
and a side-parting you could set your watch to.
A Carnforth railman's lad, hauled himself up
by his eh-bah-gum braces, grammar school,
Cambridge, millionaire, Tory MP.
Then Chairman of the Party v Arthur Scargill
on *Question Time*. King Arthur, the Cossack-quiffed
syndicalist from nah-then-lad Worsborough Dale,
President of the NUM via White Cross
Secondary Modern, Woolley Pit and the diehard
red-raggers of Yorkshire, the real Yorkshire,
where we lived, with pit tips, comprehensive schools
and sideburned Tetley bittermen,
not the sheep-spotted, cowpat Dales, beloved
of Southerners and the *Yorkshire Post*,
home of Tory farmers and fleece-topped
middle-class hikers; the *real* Yorkshire,
red or dead in tooth and claw,
in Docs and denims and donkey jackets,
the Yorkshire that flew into lines of coppers,
the Yorkshire that took down a Government;
there before us on TV, taking them down once more.
*'There are five points I'd like to make in response
to that frankly, preposterous assertion …'*
—and in our flat South Riding vowels
he reeled them off, one after the other,
fluent as the Dearne, consonants blunt
as cobbles, arguments sharp as a diamond-bit,
each word a slap in the face, a punch
to the stomach, flustering Parkinson's
brilliantined cool, stammering
his learned RP. *One of us.* Inspired,
we were off, into CND, Anti-Nazi League
and the Socialist Workers Party,
NME reading fifth-formers, fighting fascists
in Leeds, selling papers on the market corner
debating Toryboy Hague on Radio Aire,
taking to the streets in Blackpool,
Liverpool, London and Hull, for jobs,
against racism and nuclear missiles,
building barricades, daubing graffitos,
getting clubbed by the SPG: then '84,
the Alamo, labour's last stand: the call went out
and his people answered: Arthur Scargill,
we'll support you evermore.

Steve Ely

Translations From Abandoned Books

Keith Ridgway

'We have here some dangerous demonstrations of dissent and subversion and we should not stand for this nor allow them; and we should not tolerate this corruption of the public spirit nor the telling of such lies against this nation.'

Having said these words, the deputy sat back down. His face wore a grim and dignified mask. There was a little nodding. Someone, a single voice, uttered a bravo. There was however a pause—a definite uncertainty.

It was your mother who laughed first, and your father who almost immediately joined her, and in the otherwise silent chamber their laughs became infectious. First one and then a second and then a third deputy began to smile and then to laugh, and fat bellies began to bounce gently up and down, and expensively tailored suit shoulders began to rise and fall, and smiling mouths began to open and to emit, in an almost involuntary fashion, loud guffaws and peals of giggles, and soon the entire parliament rang with uproarious hilarity.

—Alberto Aquilani, *L'ultima guerra*, 1952

—

The sun over the desert is not, according to this point of view, capable of either heat or light, and the desert itself produces the sun. The sun exists, but it only exists in the desert, which cannot be said of the desert, in its relation to the sun. The desert creates the sun. Without the sun the desert is not a desert, and the apparition of Angelica Huston offering a cure tonic is impossible. The desert fulfils its particular function here—it creates everything upon it, and as such is the plateau of possibility necessary for the story to end. For the story can only end in possibility, in a widening out—something which we see literally as Neeson and Brosnan walk off in different directions. Their wounds are surely fatal, their most recent experiences are almost certainly hallucinations, and yet it is impossible to say which one of them is hallucinating the other, and whether the desert, which is the engine of this denouement, is complicit with us the witnesses, or with the protagonists, thereby making us the victims of our own hallucination, or with the sun, which would make of all of us—witnesses and protagonists alike—useless germs in the heat.

—Francesca Pasquale, *Hollywood Frainteso*, 2009

—

Her fingers, as with the levers of a terrible engine, dragged in a crawling and inexorable fashion the instrument of her hand along his naked leg, to his knee and his thigh. He could not breathe. The window filled his eyes, and he stared through its dirty glass, over her shoulder, into the smudged blue of the distant and impenetrable sky. He felt that he was not where he was. But he was not far away either. He was not, for example, in the sky. Her device encountered the material of his underpants, a thin layer of cheap blue fabric separating her knuckles from his squirming scrotum. He breathed and examined the glass that sat against the sky. The hand exerted pressure, precisely measured as if by detailed calculation, against his balls. She kissed his neck and his ear. He could smell her shampoo like metal after rain. He could feel his penis strain his underpants and he knew that it was exuding a small dark oily patch against the blue where the tip was, and he knew that he was elsewhere, not in the sky, but not here either—in just his underpants on the bed with this girl. He was in the glass. He was in the glass between the girl and the sky, and he was smudged like the glass. Her finely crafted fingers operated in accurate configuration with the outline of his half remembered fears and their psychological neighbours, his hopes, and manoeuvred their way under his balls and pressed against his body there, and his eyes closed. He was the glass.

—Daniel Zawadzki, *Chłopców I Dziewcząt*, 1976.

—

Blue container four shackled the epithrum to its flank and hovered by the gateway fin, as if observing. Texler rolled another bacusnap and inhaled deeply of its bitter-sweet smoke, closing his eyes briefly and thinking of Anna. He resisted for minutes the urge to plug into the Pool Grid to see if she was there. The remote accounter didn't show her. But it showed no one. He had, some hours before, killed himself. His suicide was blinking through the Pool like a pulsar, and his reappearance already ridiculed, condemned and accepted before he had initiated it. He thought perhaps he wouldn't, but knew he would. Anna was there. She would always be there. She would always be only there. He could travel through the night for a million years and he would never find her. He inhaled again. Only on the grid. It was the old saying. Only on the grid. He looked out at the universe. The ice steamed on the hull. A slow rotating maintenance arm reflected milky starlight. The glint in the east was a light year distant. There was nothing, nothing at all, in any direction.

—Greta Balicki, *Summa*, 2007

—

We have this extended buttress of blindness, because we can only see what is useful to us. For the arbiter of human usefulness is ribcaged and waist high, and we are not as we think we are. At least, I don't think we are. I don't understand how we could be, given everything you've done in your life. And your life is not unusual, kid, not these days. And I don't think you are uninteresting. I do not think that.

But we are busy with nothing. We are busy writing. We are busy watching each other. We are busy reading. We are busy carrying the vernacular from your father's generation to your mother's lonely brother's lost life, to the children's little universe, to the universe of dead souls and the everything of each nothing step. Each nothing step. Our lives are laid open. And we pick our way through these fields, in nothing steps, in steps that are steps because we call them steps. But the better life is hidden, kid. It is lost and it is not written down. Remember this. Always remember this. The better lives of the ones who went out to the shops and who never came back.

—Antonio Maturi, *La spalla*, 1993

—

There is a ghost train that runs through this house. The express howl of all your meetings and partings, all the faces you have ever seen, pressed to the windows of the carriages. The carriages.

—Mario Balla, *756990*, 2009

—

The dream of sublime integration with a more comfortable world of open fields and clear skies and clean water, where one may experience, if not freedom, then a feeling of freedom of movement—both literally and in the sense of one's conversation and thought and daily diversions—this dream has become mired. The skies are thunderous, the water is brackish, the fields have turned to muck. Instead of relaxation, the post communist state has introduced, of course, a febrile and all pervading competition. The threat has now become not one of potential state interference, where one might be punished for some perceived breach of law or etiquette or mere thought, but the risk of personal failure, where one might be punished for some imperceptible breach of the unwritten laws of success, aspiration, doing well, making the best of things, playing along. Playing along is common to both of these paradigms, as it is common to all. But our participation is no longer the point. It is no longer worth anything. Or, to be more precise, it is no longer worth anything to us. We cannot bargain with it. Playing at not playing along is, in the new Poland, a much more difficult role. There is no script. There is no clear model. There is no encouraging geographically located chorus of encouragement. No promised land. No West. If you choose to opt out of this game, you must find your own way. And you will not be rewarded with martyrdom or alarm or notoriety or opprobrium. You will simply be ignored. The best you can hope for is a casual dismissal. You are no longer a subversive, a freedom fighter, a dissenter. You are, at best, an eccentric. You do not threaten the game. You entertain the players. You are, in what is the most cruel appellation of this crushing neoliberal capitalism… an individual.

—Olga Dudek, *Od tego czasu Polska*, 2006

—

There was a bad smell in the alley of dogs or shit or kitchen scraps but as soon as he noticed it he placed it somewhere—somewhere else—he allocated it a place and it stayed there and did not bother him unduly. The taller boy had a small rip in the shoulder of his T-shirt where the seam had parted, and he stared at the teardrop shape of the skin there, as if there was something particular in it that he wanted, that was not available to his hands, which were on the boy's waist, on his back, beneath his T-shirt, or to his lips, which were on the boy's lips, his cheek, his neck. His eyes returned again and again to the tiny piece of skin on this shoulder. As if it was more important. The other boy, the redhead, stood back a little, an outstretched arm running a hand over the others' bodies, and he turned to him, and reached out, and pulled him to them, so that their three mouths met and kissed, and their lips hesitated in the tiny triangular space between them, and their tongues danced in the air, a trinity of desire, creating something out of the gap between them that they wanted to close because it was not possible to close it. And as soon as he had thought of that he thought of something else. A hand slipped under his waistband, touching his buttocks. That was the redhead, he thought. He shivered but it was not cold. He looked again at the tall boy's shoulder. He moved his head, bent it, bowed, and kissed that important patch of skin, as if it were a relic, a holy place. His body hummed. His tongue tasted the dry sweet important place, but it seemed not to be what he had thought it was. He felt for the tall boy's penis, felt it through the cheap rough fabric of his work trousers. He sucked his tongue and bit his lips. The redheaded boy was rushing them. The alley was patient. There was no noise but their breath, and the night. He unbuckled the boy's jeans, pushed them down, tugged at his underwear, felt his hard warm cock in his hand, squeezed it, awoke. He awoke. They were three boys in an alley. He knew it was hopeless. He knew it even as he dropped to his knees and tasted the tall boy's cock in his mouth like the taste of warm bottled water on a beach in the summer. He knew it even as he took the redhead's cock as well. He knew it as he stood and they together unclothed him and the tall boy bent and kissed his chest, his stomach, and the redheaded boy kissed his buttocks, parted them with his lips, licked his hole. He knew it all the time. He stared at the teardrop shape of skin on the tall boy's shoulder and he knew. It was hopeless.

—Daniel Zawadzki, *Chłopców I Dziewcząt*, 1976.

My visit to the house of the poet is presaged by storms and a delayed ferry, on which the smell of vomit, when it finally takes to the seas, is overpowering and yet reassuring, reminding me as it does of nature's casual dominance over us, and of our casual dominance over its recurring reminders. I recall the long work 'Legion Hall And Its Breakages', in which McLoughlin stamps his own melodramatic mark on this theme with his 'disordered lines of fluff and howlers', which ruin the new church and pin the altar boy 'beneath God's hard beam, an Isaac formless, no test this time.'

McLoughlin meets me at the door, his nearly eighty years not affecting him with much more than an attractively lined face and a slight hesitation on downhill slopes. His small cottage, warm and clean, faces south across a bare descending hill to the sea, the view spoiled only slightly by some ugly farm buildings and a scattering of sheep. The sea itself—turbulent, bruised, noisy—seems to delight him. His gaze turns to it automatically in every idle moment. All the chairs in the house seem angled towards a seaward window. His work room is lined with notebooks which he will not allow me to look at. Their spines suggest they are all the same. Whether full or empty I cannot tell. He has two dogs and a cat. There is a typewriter. There is even a small laptop computer, 'for the e-mails,' he says, and a telephone. But on his desk there are only two notebooks, a larger pad covered in doodles, and a tub full of pens and pencils. 'I work very inefficiently,' he tells me. 'I lose lines. I can spend a day looking for a line I wrote last week. And when I find it, it has changed. Of course.' He pours us some fresh coffee and offers me breakfast. I decline, and he looks crestfallen.

'You must eat,' he says. 'Look at you. You are thin as paint. Please, I have bacon, sausages. Fresh eggs from the farm. You have never tasted eggs like them. Look! Look at this bread! Baked this morning, a mile from here. I have pudding, dense black pudding like treacle. What is wrong with you? You must eat! You must!'

He is almost angry. I still feel nauseous from the ferry. I nod. He begins to cook, and soon the small steamy kitchen is filled with the smell of frying. I think of his lines in 'Potter's Last Morning', in which 'the sun fries an egg of land and sizzles the grass like rashers', and I excuse myself in search of the bathroom, but find only the front door, and the hill to the sea, and in the fresh blast of salty wind I roll down there on my own stomach like a ferret over a cliff.

In my stomach, not on.

—Nathaniel Körtig, *Die Dichter*, 2006

She pushed her cunt down on his face, and he spluttered in the near dark and nothing, he thought, could be nicer. He could not breathe. She hit his chest, or his stomach, he could not tell, and in the dark airless mush of his experience he did not care if he lived or died. No! That was not true! For it was here, in the smell and dampness of her cunt that the truth became stark and clear. Everything else was nothing. Here, smothering, was where he was truly himself, truly what he was, truly alive. And the truth was that here, with regard to the stupid argument between life and death, he sided with death, for everything about his senses was pure life. And the truth was that here, death was what he in fact desired. And the truth was that here, nothing but the smell of her piss and her cunt and her sweat and her blood existed, and it was the life of truth and nothing could come after it but the life of death.

—Mark Hellani, *Beyrouth Beyrouth alors*, 2010

The reasons I know of that we are not allowed to talk to our grandmother

Evelyn Conlon

It began with me having to do an essay for school about my grandmother. Only some of us were asked to do it. It was for a competition for a visiting writer who was coming to our class the following month.

'Is that all he does, Sir, write?'

'Yes that's what he is, a writer, just like your father is an actuary I believe.'

This may have been the first time the boy had a name for what his father was. Those of us who were chosen made a show of huffing and puffing and told the others that they were lucky, but secretly I was pleased. The essay was to be about how the old spent their Saturday nights. Mr McGrane was particularly interested in how those who lived alone fared on such a busy evening. He must have chosen those of us who had grannies living alone, maybe it was not because we were good at essays. We could concentrate on aspects of loneliness, were they more poignant in contrast to the fullness of the clamour and clatter of a Saturday night? *Poignant*. We could look it up in the dictionary. And while we were at it we could find out the difference between bathos and pathos. The ones who weren't chosen laughed at this and some of them pointed their fingers at us. Mr McGrane saw them and said that everyone had to look up the words.

'And I would like you to stick as near to the truth as possible.'

It was this commandment that made me niggle my father over and over again that evening and the next day to bring me to our grandmother's at 9 o'clock on the Saturday night. That was not a time that we would normally visit her. I had decided on 9 o'clock because I thought that the loneliness mentioned by Mr McGrane would have set in by then and I'd be able to see it for myself without my grandmother or my father knowing what I was up to.

When we arrived at the door she wasn't in and my father seemed annoyed by this. We puttered about for a while but she didn't come back.

'Are you sure Mr McGrane meant you to be so precise. Seems more like a report to me than an essay. Surely an essay should be more imaginative.'

I hated it when my father got all know-all like that. As if he knew better than my teacher. I said, bolstered by the order to accuracy, 'Yes.'

'Oh well then, we'd better look for her I suppose' my father said.

We went next door to my grandmother's neighbour, an old woman who scared me the way that I think grandmothers are maybe meant to but which mine didn't. My father asked her if she might know where my grandmother was.

'What time is it? That blooming clock is never right.'

This struck me as odd, surely there would be more than one clock in the house. Ours had at least four that I could think of at this minute. Maybe I would put in the essay that my grandmother's neighbour had only one clock which was always wrong.

'It's eh, let me see,' and my father pulled back the sleeve of his jacket to look at his watch which has a purple face. I could hear a baby crying at the house on the other side.

'Half past nine now,' he said.

'Half past nine on a Saturday night. Well, she'll have her feet well up back in Cannings by now. Cannings you know, the pub.'

My father closed his face. You have to know him well to see him doing this. I know him well, or at least the bits of him that I notice.

'Cannings, the pub,' she said again, putting the emphasis on the last word.

'Yes. Yes,' my father said, and my grandmother's neighbour chuckled.

'What did she mean *back* in Cannings?' I asked when we were in the car.

'Oh she's from the West, they say back with everything.'

My father sounded cross. I was only trying to get him to open his face again.

Maybe if we hadn't gone to the pub it would have been alright. He parked the car in a sullen manner. I would need to look that up too with the bathos word. I hear words and like them but sometimes use them in the wrong place. He said, 'Stay there,' unnecessarily. Even I knew that children were not allowed in pubs after nine o'clock at night. There had been an uproar about it which I couldn't understand. What on earth could happen that you would absolutely have to have a child in a pub after nine o'clock at night? And what was the difference between a pub and a bar? I hadn't brought my book with me, we had after all only been going to visit our grandmother. There was nothing to read in the car except some scraps but they did alright.

My father came out from the pub a few minutes later—I'm not sure exactly how long he was in there but I hadn't got bored. He was fuming. That word is definitely correct. I thought it best not to talk on the way home.

Evelyn Conlon

I was sent to bed unreasonably early. Later, as the noise from the kitchen got louder I left my room and sat on the top of the stairs. There is always a child on the stairs, otherwise how would we learn.

'You want to see the crowd she was with.'

'Did you know *any* of them?'

'Not one. And the way she…'

'Tell me again what she said,' my mother interrupted, sounding as if she wanted to put the answer out flat on the table and examine it the way she does when she sews something.

'She said that I should be grateful she had a life and wasn't sitting at home alone moping about. She said that I had no business checking up on her, that she'd had enough constriction when she was rearing me.'

'Are you sure it was constriction she said?'

'Yes I'm sure,' my father ground out, 'I would hardly make it up.'

'And did she really ask you to leave?' my mother asked in her kind voice.

'Well, as good as.'

The conversation went on like this for a long time, sounding liked turned-down music or faraway wind, but I couldn't follow it really and also I did get bored because I couldn't understand what they were getting so exercised about. You can use that word as a description. It does not mean that they have been running or swimming all night.

On Monday when Mr McGrane asked me how the essay was going I said, 'Fine.'

It was very soon after this, maybe Wednesday, that my grandmother arrived at our house full of high dudgeon—I love when I can think that's what people are in. I'm almost certain that if the pub episode had not happened we would not have got that visit. This time I was out in the garden, and although my father closed the door—now that I think of it already not prepared to let things return to normal, geared up for a shouting match—I moved up to the back wall and sat down under the open window. My older sister was getting married next year I think. There was a lot of fuss, even already, I'd heard my mother saying. Sometimes it would last for an entire hour but then it would die down for days. Sometimes there would be the word wedding wedding blowing up all over the place. And then there would be weeks when no one at all mentioned the caravan as my mother called it. I didn't care about the ins and outs of it, but I presumed it would be interesting to be a part of it on the actual day. It was also a very long way away so I could see no reason to think about it yet. So it surprised me that our grandmother arrived so early to discuss it. Although I'm sure this could not really be called a discussion.

'As you are well aware I have no interest in ribbons so clearly I'll be having some trouble with this,' my grandmother said. She must then have thrown something on the table, a letter or a card. I don't know if she gave my parents time to finish reading it—there was quiet for a very short time.

'Now I know that there are sewers in the world, people who sew'—even I knew that this was a dig at my mother—'but they don't have to stick needles into everything.'

'Just a minute,' my father said.

'Yes,' my grandmother said, letting the word turn up at the end, as if it was a question or being said by an Australian.

'Just a minute,' my father repeated, 'this is no way to talk to my wife.'

'Oh for heaven's sake, Liam, your what, she has a name, and actually I'm not just talking to Gertrude, I'm talking to you too. You may not be allowed to say that your daughter has lost the complete run of herself but I can. I will not, I repeat will not, be told by anyone what to wear and no one will ask me to put a ribbon on a hat. Who said I was going to wear a hat anyway?'

'I don't think she meant it like that,' my mother said.

'And may I ask what way you think she meant it? This is quite clear. An order to wear a specific colour so that I can fit into some ludicrous pattern which this young one has in mind.'

'But is there anything wrong with the colours matching on the day?' my mother asked.

My father had gone quiet.

'No indeed there's not, if it so happens that they do. But that's the point, if it so happens.'

Clearly our grandmother was trying to show some interest but I could tell that she didn't care about colours at all. And just then my father piped up, 'This isn't about colours at all, is it mother? This is about your attitude to marriage.'

Whoa, that was some leap.

I could feel the silence outside and the leg that was under my other one went funny.

'Maybe you're right,' my grandmother finally said. 'If you must know, and I think you're old enough now to be able to bear it, I do have serious difficulties with marriage. I think it's something that should be done privately and not particularly referred to again unless legally necessary.'

She sounded as if she was on a home run.

'If you remember I never referred to your father as my husband until he died, and if you'll care to remember, this had no bearing on what I felt about or for him.'

'Your trouble is that you have no respect for tradition…' my father said.

'Tradition my arse…'

'Look there's no need to be so rude.'

'Oh grow up, that's not being rude.'

It was funny hearing someone tell my father to grow up. I had to scratch myself so that I wouldn't be found under the window.

There was a moment's silence, as if my grandmother realised the futility of it all. I had looked up 'futility' the night before. It sounded too as if they were all waiting to see who would go next.

My mother then said, 'Could you not just…' but my grandmother interrupted in a soft voice, 'No I could not just anything. This is what principle means. Someone has to stand up to this…'

She didn't finish the sentence, as if even she knew that the next word out of her mouth could be too crucial.

'And as for tradition, these days anything can be made up into it. It could be something started five years ago. Any old gobshite in a bar could tell them it was always done and they'd believe him.'

'You'd know all about that.'

I didn't know if it was fair of my father to say that. My grandmother then changed her voice into the sort of a one that my mother sometimes uses on us, only us. It comes from outside the sound of normal conversation.

'In this tradition of yours,' my grandmother said, 'I see that maternal respect has got the push.'

It sounded as if she was just at the beginning of her sentence but my father interrupted in the voice that he uses on the telephone if someone rings from work—everyone was changing voices now—'I'm sorry you feel like that. Do you want a lift anywhere?'

I could hear him coming towards the window so I had to crouch my way across to the hedge and slip behind the coal shed away out of sight. It's not used as a coal shed any more since we got the natural gas. Everything is thrown into it. I didn't hear the car leaving.

At teatime the faces were all closed.

And that night when I went out on the stairs I could hear a real dingdust of a shouting match. When their voices get that way they wouldn't notice me even if they tripped over me. The shoutings all ran into each other and it was hard to make out where one began and the other ended, but I did hear plainly my mother saying, 'Your mother was always the same. Happy away up there on her high horse. I'm not surprised she has ended up…' I couldn't hear the next bit.

'And as for these views of hers. Always superior in her mind to everyone else. Could never have the same look on things as everyone else. Oh no, Miss Precious.'

She was talking about my grandmother!

'There was no call for that, no call at all,' my father shouted.

I had to agree with him. I heard a door slamming, saw a slice of light land on the banisters and knew that someone was going to make towards the hall and in truth too I had decided that it was best for me to hear no more anyway. I slid my bottom across the linoleum into my bedroom. My mother had changed all the upstairs carpet for linoleum—I liked the colour of that word—she said it was healthier. You could never tell the connections that some people make, they must think a lot to come up with them.

The following weekend I was taken away by my parents to the west and we all had a very smooth time, people holding hands and all that.

On Monday Mr McGrane asked me how the essay was going and I said, 'Fine, Sir.'

He also said that in the opinion of some Wittgenstein tried to destroy philosophy because he could not understand it. He added: 'There is no point in destroying something if you don't know what it is. Then again for many that's why they destroy things, precisely because they do not know their worth. I hope you got that. Some of you may need to know it. And he destroyed Mr Russell too.'

Whoever he was.

I am already a perhaps sort of person. Perhaps everything would have gone completely back to normal if my essay had not won the competition. And been printed in the local paper. Oh shite. I can say that out loud because my parents seem to have too much else on their minds to notice and to reprimand me. I got a postcard from my grandmother congratulating me and this seems to have let all hell loose altogether. But my father did say yesterday, 'See, I told you an imaginative approach would have been better.' The fact that he referred to it at all makes me think that his face might open again and that I'll be able to speak to my grandmother some day.

Chronic City

by Jonathan Lethem (Faber & Faber, 2009, £14.99)

The Unnamed

by Joshua Ferris (Viking Penguin, 2010, £12.99)

The contemporary American novel has an identifiable default mode. It tends towards the quirky, the whimsically inventive. It observes with suspicion the hegemonic shenanigans of the corporate mass media. It regards with fatalistic scorn the capitalist excesses of the failing American Empire. It is fond of tricksy narrators who undergo picaresque adventures. The protagonist of Jonathan Safran Foer's *Extremely Loud and Incredibly Close* (2005), for example, is a nine-year-old genius whose father has been killed in the World Trade Centre attacks. These are cartoonish books, books in which everything is already in quotes, books that are constantly hedging their bets. We aren't writing realistic novels, goes the argument—we're writing cartoons, because isn't the world around us, with its informational overload and its dwindling moral sense, a kind of monstrous cartoon?

Jonathan Lethem's *Chronic City* and Joshua Ferris's *The Unnamed* are exemplars of the breed. In *Chronic City*, a former child actor, living in Manhattan, befriends an eccentric failed rock critic who is obsessed with purchasing a kind of magical goblet (a 'chaldron'). In *The Unnamed*, a lawyer suffers from a disease that compels him to walk until he collapses from exhaustion. Both books take place in heightened versions of contemporary America, besieged (in the Ferris) by eruptions of freak weather or (in the Lethem) by an escaped tiger of exaggerated size. Superficially dissimilar, these two novels in fact tell us the same thing about the real subject of contemporary American fiction, which is anxiety.

Both Ferris and Lethem are anxious writers—not in the sense that they write about anxiety (although they do), but in the sense that they are anxious, often to a fault, about one of the most basic constituent parts of the novel as a form: character. This is, of course, a legacy of postmodernism, which has had a long and baleful influence on American fiction; and indeed, both *Chronic City* and *The Unnamed* are solidly, dutifully postmodern. The anxiety they exhibit is a specifically postmodern anxiety, and it has to do with fiction and human character; with what Virginia Woolf once described as the relationship between Mr Bennett and Mrs Brown.

Anxiety—about genre, form, but especially character—has marked Jonathan Lethem's fiction from the start. The things you remember from his books are not characters, but gimmicks. *Motherless Brooklyn* (1999) is narrated by a private detective who suffers from Tourette's Syndrome. *The Fortress of Solitude* (2003) features a magic ring that confers invisibility. And Lethem's most recent book, the disappointing *You Don't Love Me Yet* (2007), involves a failed indie rock band, an art installation that parodies telephone helplines, and a kidnapped kangaroo.

Lethem's work doesn't lack for inventiveness. His prose, too, is rhythmic and richly various—reading him can feel like reading a paranoid, trippy Saul Bellow who happens to be obsessed with pop-culture trivia. But when it comes to character, he is helplessly trapped in the mode of the caricaturist. And in this, he is representative of a whole generation of American novelists who have inherited a postmodern anxiety about the self—and hence about character in fiction.

Character names are one giveaway. Lethem has been sweating over his: Perkus Tooth, Chase Insteadman, Laird Noteless. These names work the way names work in Dickens: they signal that we are in a world of crotchets and caricatures, a world in which selfhood is reducible to a collection of quirks and comic tics. Perkus Tooth, the failed rock critic, is obsessed with minor filmmakers, obscure bands, and of course his chaldrons. (He also smokes am unbelievable amount of weed. With *Chronic City*, Lethem has managed to smuggle a stoner novel into the mainstream of American literature—just as Seth MacFarlane, the creator of *Family Guy*, has managed to smuggle a stoner show onto a major American network.)

Like Perkus, Chase Insteadman—the narrator of *Chronic City*—is a caricature. He lives on residuals from a sitcom he starred in as a child. His fiancée, Janice Trumbull, is trapped in a space station orbiting the earth. He is unencumbered by real pain, real experience. He is free to cruise around Lethem's chronic city, directing us from one comic riff to the next. He is also, in human terms, a vacuum. He has no interiority to speak of. His friends are freaks, distinguishable from one another only by their obsessions. Chase's interiority—which consists of his ambivalence about Janice and his fascination with Perkus Tooth—is a joke. And it is meant to be a joke: Lethem cannot offer us a believable human being as a protagonist, because, for him, the whole notion of 'a believable human being' is already in quotes, hopelessly inaccessible behind layers of postmodern irony. Lethem's anxiety about the self has seeped into his art, and it has left his fictional landscapes barren. As Virginia Woolf writes in 'Mr Bennett and Mrs Brown' (published, mind you, in 1923): 'It is because this essence, this character-making power, has evaporated that novels are for the most part the soulless bodies we know, cumbering our tables and clogging our minds.'

The problems besetting Joshua Ferris's *The Unnamed* are in the same ballpark.

It is to Ferris's credit that his protagonist is more or less an ordinary man: he even goes by the impeccably Everymanish name of Tim Farnsworth, so we know we're not quite in Lethemland just yet. *The Unnamed* (the title, of course, alludes to *The Unnameable* by Samuel Beckett) is Ferris's second novel—in 2007 he published the extraordinary *Then We Came to the End*, a small masterpiece of observational comedy written in a miraculously sustained first-person-plural voice. And Ferris's follow-up is, despite numerous flaws, a resonant and moving allegory about man's estate, in which Tim Farnsworth's 'idiopathic' disease comes to stand for all disease, and ultimately for the final sickness from which none of us recover.

Ferris has attempted a simplified third-person prose in *The Unnamed*, but his ear has deserted him. On the first page, we get: 'a grudging towards the burden of adjustment' —and there are many more such syntactical abominations littering the novel. The other major difficulty is Ferris's decision to place his suffering Everyman in a kind of alternate USA, in which weather conditions have become unpredictably hostile.

The freak-weather stuff—as well as provoking some of Ferris's worst prose—detracts from the power of the novel's central conceit. Why does Tim Farnsworth have to live in a fantastical America, full of weird snows and sudden storms? Wouldn't his predicament be more resonant and horrifying if he lived in the world we know? But such is Ferris's anxiety about writing 'realistic' fiction that he is compelled to abandon the fine-grained, lyric attentiveness to the everyday that made his first novel so wonderful.

Both Lethem and Ferris are gifted novelists. But until they stop blundering around in the dead ends of postmodernism, their work will be hobbled by the anxieties of a previous generation. The world may be a monstrous cartoon, but the people who live in it are still, the last time I checked, real people—believable human beings, if you will. Contemporary novelists should remember this—and remind us.

—KEVIN POWER

Hand in the Fire

by Hugo Hamilton (Fourth Estate, 2010, £12.99)

Dublin writer Hugo Hamilton's new novel *Hand in the Fire* is a conversation with the dead; those within us, beyond us and who continue to haunt us, demanding to be remembered, and calling us towards responsibility and transformation. Hamilton, the son of an Irish father and a German mother, has previously examined the complexities of identity, place and cultural difference in two memoirs, including *The Speckled People* (2003), seven novels and a collection of short stories. These key themes are again at the centre of his latest work.

The novel tells the tale of Vid Cosic, a young Serbian immigrant living in Celtic Tiger Ireland, and explores the difficulties in trying to adapt and settle into a new place that isn't home. It opens with the return of a lost mobile phone and with that the beginning of a friendship between Vid and a young Dublin lawyer called Kevin Concannon. From the outset, Hamilton establishes the fragility of communication and the slippage between understanding and misunderstanding. As Kevin tells Vid, 'there was a secret language here, not the old, Irish language or the English language, but something in between the lines, like a code.' It is a misunderstanding of this code that eventually leads to the lengthy and far-reaching consequences of a brutal attack on a work night out and sees Vid taking the blame for Kevin's barbaric violence, as well as tests in full the saying that provides the inspiration for Hamilton's title: 'A true friend was somebody who would put his hand in the fire for you.' The friendship that unfolds is an umbrageous web of uncertainty, complicity, secrecy and silence. However, it would be too simple to suggest that the friendship that develops between the two solely relies on Vid taking the blame for Kevin's attack. Throughout the novel Hamilton interrogates the limits and the depths of friendship. He writes: 'Nobody does friendship like you do in this country. It comes out of nowhere. Full on. All or nothing. I've been to places where friendship is cultivated with great care over a longer period of time, like a balcony garden. Here it seems to grow wild.'

Hamilton is at his best when he is dealing with the vulnerability of his main characters both of whom are haunted by ghosts and memories which punctuate the present with pangs of despair and sharp unease. Vid struggles with his lapsed memory of the war and the death of his parents in a car crash while Kevin and the rest of the Concannon family must confront their memories of an absent father. History and place are presented as estranging, broadening and darkening spaces with the most poignant absence and haunting of self, place and identity captured in the drowning of the ancestral Máire Concannon, the drowned woman or the bean báite. The Connemara woman is denounced by her local priest for falling pregnant out of wedlock. From the altar, 'The priest had put it to the men in the congregation to drown her. Because every man in the whole of Connemara was under suspicion while she was walking around with a baby in her belly and no husband by her side. And if they were not men enough to do that and clear their own names, so the story went, she should have the decency to drown herself.' Hamilton's powerful evocation of transgression, community, violence and sacrifice in the name of place, religion or nation-state is captured in this woman's history. His depiction of Connemara, Forba and the Aran Islands evoke this unrelenting hold of the past on the present as well. However, the attempt to juxtapose twenty-first century Ireland with its own past and to echo it with the trauma of the Balkan War is less successful and, to say the least, slightly arrogant and naïve. Hamilton's attempt to find a universal history of mourning and trauma ultimately fails. As Vid tours Ireland taking in the sights at Dursey Island, Howth, Dun Laoghaire, Belfast and Carrick-on-

Shannon it feels as though one is reading the *Rough Guide to Ireland*. From the Howth of Joyce and Nora to the Belfast of the Troubles, Hamilton's attempt to bridge place and history within the novel reads more as artifice than truth.

The success of *Hand in the Fire* is its reflection on the folding of time and memory. Mourning and the past darken the present of those who bear the scars of loss. As the philosopher Jacques Derrida has written of time and the unconscious, it 'makes us concerned not with horizons of modified-past or future-presents but with a "past" that has never been present, and which never will be, whose future to come will never be a production of a reproduction in the form of the presence.' Hamilton, in his latest novel, is attempting to deal with this complexity of time, showing how the past intrudes upon the present, making it both fractured and unstable. He suggests that perhaps it is indeed possible to transcend the past and to rewrite painful histories in a continuous production of life. However, this futurity depends on both individual and collective mourning, where grief and the loss of home, family and friendships are not laid to rest but instead are recognised and brought into the present, albeit in new and transformative ways.

—MARIA PARSONS

Identity Parade: New British and Irish Poets

Edited by Roddy Lumsden (Bloodaxe, 2010, £12.00)

Poetry anthologies are often sectarian documents designed to raise the status of one or other poetry trend at the expense of others that are carefully excluded. The well-known *Best of American Poetry* annuals, for example, have sometimes been used as strategic weapons in the fractious long game of Anglophone poetry. The hugely influential critic and canon-guard Harold Bloom famously used the introduction to his 1999 volume of the series to rubbish the work of Adrienne Rich and Identity Poetics in general.

In his own *Identity Parade* the London-based Scottish poet-editor Roddy Lumsden attempts something different, providing readers with a kind of aerial map of contemporary Anglo-Irish poetry which reveals where the mainstream of poetry has clustered over the last two decades as well as showing a certain amount of its edgelands and other territories. In his brisk introduction Lumsden rejects outright the traditional generational anthologiser's prerogative to establish or buttress an emergent canon but speaks instead of a desire to 'spread the word, educate, recommend' and to highlight the work of the 'undersung'. This inclusivity testifies to the massive reading job Lumsden has had to undertake for the book—over a thousand poets came within its terms of reference. Perhaps it is also his attempt to predict or even influence the future courses of the art. In any case the book is enriched by his decision to highlight what he calls 'the plural now'. Very few readers, no matter how particular or genre-bound their poetic tastes, will find nothing to please or surprise them in *Identity Parade.*

Proceedings open promisingly with an energetic and accessible selection from premier league slammer Patricia Agbagi. Later on Tim Turnbull and Kevin Higgins are among those who display the rich and meaningful music that comes through to poetry when, as Willam Carlos Williams put it 'Ear and eye lie down in bed together'. As Lumsden points out, the poetry reading and festival culture is currently thriving and, despite the often cranky rejection of street poetry and performance aesthetics from within the academic establishment, some of the best work by the university based poet-critics herein (one third of the book's poets are academics) does show an increased structural and thematic awareness of a listening and live audience as well as of the silent, atomised and distant-in-time-and space reader—who might as well be called God, or Harold—to which poetry with canonical ambitions is often addressed. Essex university's Andy Brown playfully intertextual 'A Poem of Gifts' enscapsulates well this incipient crossover between higher-educated polysemy and streetwise orality.

The post-avant is also represented. Peter Manson's dense, charged post-Mallarmian canvases are both imagistically and acoustically evocative enough to provoke obsessive re-readings from this reader at least. Meanwhile, Matthew Whelton's marriage of Oulipian constrained writing techniques with populist subject matter in 'An ABC of American Suicide' is perhaps the most successful modal fusion in the book. A certain amount of hybridity and open form is evident in much of the work on display, though nowhere near what is to be found in contemporary music or visual arts.

Lumsden has also chosen the unusual and daring course of including a number of poets who have yet to publish. This risk is justified in the case of regular *Stinging Fly* contributor Ailbhe Darcy, whose provocative 'Crossing' is easily the volume's standout travel poem. Thanks in part, I guess, to Ryanair and the gap year there are lots and lots of travel poems in *Identity Parade*, though few of them perform and stimulate as well as Darcy's. Other prevalent themes here include childhood and ancestors, eccentric English characters, personal relationships, exotic or endangered animals and complicated recipes. Reading *Identity Parade* is sometimes like being couched in front of Channel 4 on Wednesday evenings, before the watershed.

Identity Parade can be read to a certain extent, as I am certain Lumsden and Bloodaxe wish it to be read, as a polemic against sectarianism in poetry. However Lumsden's claims to plurality—supported by the inclusion of a majority of women poets—are seriously undermined by the volume's Londoncentrism. Thirty-nine out of seventy-six poets who mention their geography live, have worked or studied in London and there are dozens of poems which treat the people, places and things of London, making *Identity Parade* feel at times like a prolonged advert for the London Tourist Board. It is certainly an advert for the London poetry scene. Even if we accept that London is the centre of the our publishing industry, this weighting is obviously wholly disproportionate and the book is marked, with striking exceptions such as Dajit Nagra, by a distinct lack of linguistic and tonal variety as a result. Many write in a mutually intelligible poetic register that draws on a highly refined and somewhat exclusive version of British-English.

The poems here are nearly all beautiful in the sense that are very well-sculpted and clearly and sonorously expressed. Sometimes, however, when confronted with such apparent technical faultlessness, I am put in mind of Ron Silliman's question of 'what is more deadly than a poem that seeks to be told it is beautiful'. What I find lacking are formal and thematic reflections of our commonly experienced fragmentation, confusion, disturbance, upset, instability and insecurity. By and large, the senses of all-prevailing danger, irredeemable human failure and imminent total disaster that characterise the zeitgeist are not well communicated here, though they are gestured at, somewhat derivatively, in the works of Jacob Polley, who makes a parrot of Ted Hughes' 'Crow', and Paul Batchelor, the strangely legitimate son of that tongue-twisted carouser Barry MacSweeney.

For my no-money, David Wheatley is the most perceptive and well-expressed of the university oriented poets. His work is the clearest evidence here of the desperate post-historical, post-ideological, post-conviction condition afflicting our intelligentsia. Wheatley shows well what happens when one keeps the rhymes (mostly internal) but gives up on hope, as well as history, when, as he writes elsewhere 'there is no urgent reason for going on'. Claire Pollard is another whose works are admirably bleak, and far more anxious.

I do not find it credible that no Irish poetry publishers aside from Gallery (four poets out of eighty-five) and Salmon (one) have published new poetry of high standards and collectible interest in the last two decades. No British based and versed editor, no matter how much of a polymath, could have either the ear or the comprehension to take in the variety of distinct pronunciations and meanings made use of by the Hiberno-English poet. The bilingualism and exploration of liminal Englishes which are among the most noteworthy features of contemporary Hiberno-English poetry do not get a slot in this parade. An anthology of this period of Irish poetry without Gearoid MacLochlainn, to mention only the most accomplished of the absentees, is far from comprehensive.

The eerie near-total abscence of political poetry (or as Christoper Ricks put it in his recent introduction to Carcanet's *Collected Austin Clarke* of 'poetry written politically') in our era of neo-imperialism, neo-liberalism, and climate change is also deeply troubling, but not surprising. The cultural and intellectual scene overall is far less radical and interesting than it was even twenty years ago and it is apt that the general retreat from commitment and strong ideas, and concurrently from passion, risk and invention, should be reflected in poetry.

It is just as well then that Lumsden's demotic impulses have led him to include the few motley independents whose work shines through the cracks of the quietist lyrical-narrative monolith that forms the bulk of *Identity Parade*. Otherwise this book would only have served to prove that we are living in the safest and most uneventful poetic period since the long interregnum that lasted from the European deaths of Byron and Shelley until symbolism came to shore in the backwash of the revolutionary decadence of the continent more than half a century later. Overall 'the plural now', looks decidedly jaded and homogenous by comparison with any previous twenty-year period going right back to Victoria's reign.

Like planet Earth may someday hopefully be, this book is saved by its extremes. We should be grateful to Lumsden for giving them a rare but much needed airing.

—DAVE LORDAN

The Fall

by Anthony Cronin (New Island, 2010, €9.99)

Writing of Yeats and the struggle Irish poets allegedly underwent to escape his long shadow, Anthony Cronin says, 'Speaking as one who began to write, or at least to publish in the late forties I can only say that I never felt it.' This was a lucky break as anyone who has ploughed through early Philip Larkin will be only too aware. Even Auden had the problem to tackle though he found his own manner quickly enough and repaid the debt, however slight, with one of the great elegies of the last century. While acknowledging Kavanagh's genius, Cronin could no more go the peasant route than linger in the Cultic Twalette, hence the now familiar colloquial urban/urbane manner that makes him a sort of honorary member of the famously non-existent 'Movement.' His is a mind well stocked with the intellectual furniture which makes a good blaze as Kavanagh said of Auden.

This slim late flowering (the twelfth collection since the emergence of *Poems* in 1958) finds him in pensive, if not vacant mood, as history and politics, once major concerns (Anthony Burgess considered that 'The End of the Modern World' should be as well known as 'The Waste Land') are replaced by meditations on women, the Fall and a spot of God bothering ('Christmas Letter to God the Father' and 'On the Death of an Auschwitz Survivor').

Women don't come out of it particularly well and God it seems could do with pulling his socks up. While we await the prime mover's reaction with interest, this poem:

> Of course God is a woman
> God has no sense of justice or fair play
> God is not logical
> God never listens to what you say

... went over like a Hunky Dory poster when I ran it past a group of women recently.

One forms the impression reading these poems that Cronin's idea of a good night out would be a couple of drinks with Kingsley Amis and the author of Ecclesiastes. 'Misapprehensions,' which begins with the memorable line, 'Every woman worries about her bottom,' is unlikely to recruit many female fans either. Well, Cronin is no stranger to controversy and for all I know may consider that women's bottoms in recent Irish verse (as on a Hunky Dory poster) have been insufficiently covered. Another acerb is reserved for people who go about in helicopters. When you hear one it seems you seldom look up, and if you think at all what you think is: 'There goes another rich bore/ On his way to some awful club.'

Well, apart from the facts that all rich men are not bores, nor all clubs awful, if you thought or even looked up you might imagine a traffic copter or even someone being flown to hospital. But then as the late Sean MacReamoinn remarked on his eightieth birthday to the present reviewer, 'If you can't be a grumpy old ______ at my age when can you be?'

In 'Stevie' (which could almost be an outtake from Cronin's justly lauded memoir *Dead as Doornails*) we encounter the following:

> She was a bit like the Albert Hall: a curiosity
> But formidable and destined to last.
> And, having embarked on metaphors, she was like a bird.
> Yes, loveable, beaked and a little alien.

Well, yes, except that a simile isn't a bit like a metaphor, something you'd expect someone, an editor perhaps, to spot.

Anyway, what's the good news? There is life in the old land dog yet. Thomas Kinsella wrote of Cronin's first collection: 'In a world of debased standards we can't afford to ignore what is truly said, and in this small book there are at least half a dozen poems which are worth the entire life's work of the average reviewer.' Are there as many in this one then? Three candidates occur at once: the four line 'Death,' terse as Housman, chilly as Hardy, cheerful as Beckett; 'Conflict' whose grim concluding line serves to remind us how funny the author can be when he tries and, above all, the final poem, 'Birthday Thoughts.' As Camus has noted, 'Those who write obscurely have great luck: they will have commentators. The others will only have readers, and this it seems, is worthy of scorn.' It is not.

Cronin doesn't do symbols. (For a lively excoriation of academic so-called exegesis consult his essay, 'The Advent of Bloom,' in the 1982 collection *Heritage Now*.) But faced with the big question he comes up with something suspiciously like one, finding in his own cloud of unknowing, if not a silver lining, then a glimpse of gold:

> I stare at the wall of the front yard
> Which has a brief patch of sunlight on it.
> Not much, you may say.
> Not as good as the Atlantic distances
> And the metaphors and the connections,
> But in its way convincing enough.
> And anyway, it will have to do.

If this is an epiphany what is shown forth? The transcendent in the transient or Browning's 'sunset touch?' Euripedes' 'path where no man thought'? Or an unrueful resignation, a stoic acceptance that 'life is tough, but look at the alternative'?

Oddly there is almost a reprise here of an image from Cronin's first book:

> The chances of a match-stick on a stream
> An area of sunlight on a wall
> These are the things I see although I know
> They will not do for travellers' tales at all.

The work returns (by a commodious vicus of recirculation) into a circle. Mehr licht, Mr Cronin, mehr licht.

—TOM MATHEWS

Tom Cleary was born in Clonmel and educated at University College Dublin. He has worked as a teacher in London, Manchester and Leeds, and studied at Bradford University. He lives now in Hebden Bridge in the Pennines.

Evelyn Conlon was born in County Monaghan and lives in Rathmines. She is the author of three novels, her most recent being *Skin of Dreams* (Brandon, 2003). Her latest collection of short stories, *Telling: New and Selected Stories*, was published by Blackstaff. She has compiled and edited four other books. She will give the 2010 Address at the Sydney Famine Memorial this autumn.

Mary Costello is originally from Galway. Her stories were published in the anthologies *Voices: One* edited by Gus Martin and *The Hennessy Book of New Irish Writing*. Her story 'The Patio Man' was shortlisted for a Hennessy Award. She is working on a collection of stories and on a novel.

Michael Cronin teaches in Dublin City University and is Irish Language Literature Adviser to the Arts Council. His most recent work, co-edited with Peadar Kirby and Debbie Ging, *Transforming Ireland: Challenges, Critiques, Resources* was published by Manchester University Press.

Leona Cully was born in Uranium City, Canada, a mining town which no longer exists. She grew up in the midlands, in Delvin, Co. Westmeath which does still exist. Leona lives in Dublin, and recently completed the first A New Way to Fly novel writing workshop.

Steve Ely is an English writer from the Osgoldcross Wapentake in the West Riding of Yorkshire. His poem, 'Objective One,' won the Raise Your Banners political poetry competition (Bradford) in 2009. He is currently working on *Englaland*, an epic poem about England and the English and *Ratmen*, a novel.

Alyn Fenn has been writing since 2005. She has had poems published in *SHOp* poetry magazine, *Acumen, Stony Thursday*, and *Borderlines*. She has been shortlisted for and won a number of short story competitions including the People's College 2006-07, Wicklow Writers 2007, and the 2007 William Trevor Short Story competition.

Deirdre Gleeson lives in Dublin. She has previously had a story published in the Stinging Fly anthology *Let's Be Alone Together*.

Nicola Griffin lives in East Clare with her husband and two dogs. Her poems have appeared in *The Sunday Tribune, Crannóg and Ropes*. She has an MA in Writing from NUI Galway.

Stephen Devereux grew up in Suffolk and was a factory and farm worker before going to UEA as a mature student. He has taught and lectured in the North West and has published critical essays, short stories and poetry in British, Irish, American and Austrian journal and magazines.

Desmond Hogan has published five novels and four collections of stories. *Old Swords and Other Stories* was published by Lilliput Press in 2009.

Joseph Horgan was born in Birmingham, England, to Irish parents. Previously shortlisted for a Hennessy Award and a past winner of the Patrick Kavanagh Award, his first collection, *Slipping Letters Beneath the Sea*, was published by Doghouse in 2008. *The Song at your Backdoor*, a book about place and landscape, was published by Collins Press in 2010.

John Kenny is John McGahern Lecturer in Creative Writing at NUI Galway where he is director of the BA with Creative Writing. He is author of *John Banville* (Irish Academic Press, 2009) and editor of *The John McGahern Yearbook*. He is working on a collection of stories and a novel.

Edward Lee lives in Galway. His debut poetry collection, *Playing Poohsticks On Ha'penny Bridge*, was published last year by Spider Press. His second collection *Sleep* is due from the same publisher in 2011.

Aifric Mac Aodha's first poetry collection, *Gabháil Syrinx*, has just been published by An Sagart. Her poems have been published in various journals, including *Poetry Ireland Review*, *Innti* and *Bliainiris*. She has received a number of prizes for her poetry and was recently awarded an Arts Council bursary. [**Denise Blake**'s second collection, *How to Spin Without Getting Dizzy* is published by Summer Palace Press (June 2010). She is a regular contributor to Sunday Miscellany RTE Radio One and her work is included in four Sunday Miscellany anthologies. Some of her translations are included in *By the Hearth in Mín a'Leá* (Arc publications).]

Dave Lordan's second poetry collection, *Invitation to a Sacrifice*, is released by Salmon this July.

Tom Mathews' collection, *The Owl and The Pussycat*, was published by Dedalus Press in 2009.

Lynsey May lives, loves and writes in Scotland. Her scribblings, however, have found an online home at www.lynseymay.com. Her story, 'Dreamless,' was published in *The Stinging Fly* Issue 14 Volume Two (Winter 2009 – 2010).

Andrew Meehan lives and works in Galway. He was the winner of the 2010 New Writing Award at the Cúirt International Literary Festival.

Maria Parsons lectures in the Institute of Art, Design and Technology, Dun Laoghaire. She received her PhD in English literature and Film in 2009 from Trinity College, Dublin. Her thesis was entitled *The Menstruous Monstrous: Female Blood in Horror*. Her current research is on martyrdom and shamanism.

Kevin Power is the author of *Bad Day in Blackrock* (Simon & Schuster) and the winner of the 2009 Rooney Prize for Irish Literature. His short stories have appeared in *The Stinging Fly* and *These Are Our Lives* (Stinging Fly Press). He is the winner of a Hennessy XO Emerging Fiction Award for his short story 'The American Girl.' He lives in Dublin.

Keith Ridgway is a Dublin writer currently living in London. He is the author of the novels *Animals*, *The Parts* and *The Long Falling*. His next book *Hawthorn And Child* will be published in the future.

Lorna Shaughnessy was born in Belfast. She lives in Galway and lectures in Spanish in NUIG. Her first collection *Torching the Brown River* was published by Salmon Poetry in 2008. Her work was included in *The Forward Book of Poetry 2009*. In 2006 she published translations of Mexican poets Pura Lopez Colome and Maria Baranda with Arlen House.

Declan Sweeney is from east Galway. He has published poetry and prose in various periodicals in Ireland, England, and America. His writing has also been broadcast and produced on stage. 'Feast Days' is the title story of a new collection.